Any Witch Way You Can
Rachel Rawlings

This is dedicated to the one I love...

Any Witch Way You Can

Her only hope is dark magic...

Ellie James may be a powerful witch but she knows nothing—literally. Not even the simplest spell.

Her potions? So-so. Her tarot readings? Meh. If not for her (former) foster sister, Pru, sneaking her food, Ellie would have to eat her car—which would be bad, since it's also her house.

But when Pru runs away and Ellie's former foster mom shows up on Ellie's figurative doorstep, desperate for help, Ellie learns the only thing worse than knowing nothing is dealing with the witch who knows everything...

"**O**ne card draw today, Sam?" I brushed off the layer of pollen coating the weathered concrete chess table before I set my tarot deck down. "Or have I finally convinced you to get a full reading?" The question was almost rhetorical. Despite my hopes he would take the full reading and put a few extra bills in my pocket, I already knew his answer.

"One card draw." Sam's lips turned up in an easy smile, fine lines forming as it reached his tired eyes. "Like always."

"Like always." My stomach grumbled its displeasure over his answer.

Sam pulled his card and set it down next to the dysfunctional timer. "The tower? Again?" His calloused hand hovered over the five-dollar bill he'd slapped down on the table, as if considering taking it back.

"What can I say?" I shrugged. "We're in Mercury retrograde. You're going to have to deal with this stuff, Sam, or you'll pull that card every time."

The truth was it could have been me as much as Mercury retrograde. My magic was hit or miss – usually miss. But my customers didn't know that. With the exception of Sam, they wanted a little direction or affirmation they were on the right path. But Sam? He wanted a miracle.

And I wasn't in that line of work.

Sam got up from the metal stool anchored to the ground with a harrumph but he left the five.

"Thank you, Sam." I called after him. "See you next week?"

He replied with an undignified one finger salute.

"You can't please them all," I muttered to myself, shoving the day's haul – a measly eighteen dollars – into the back pocket of my jeans before collecting the seven clementines I'd taken in trade for another reading from the other end of the chess table. "At least I won't get scurvy."

A light spring breeze carried the scents of hot dogs, buttered popcorn, and sticky sweet cotton candy. None of those things ranked on my list of favorite foods to eat but my mouth watered nonetheless. I preferred steak to boiled, processed meat, no matter how many condiments you slathered on top. Champagne tastes, beer budget. I started off in the direction of the hot dog vendor. It wasn't filet mignon but it wasn't a clementine, either.

You don't have the money to spare, Ellie. I stopped short of getting line, kicking the toe of my shoe in the dirt. *Prue will be here tomorrow, with more supplies. Just like every Tuesday.* My younger sister – foster sister actually – had been sneaking food and toiletries into the park for months, ever since my foster parents kicked me out. Not everyone was as excited as Prue to find out I was gifted.

The carousel's busy season was just kicking off – and hopefully so was mine. Things could turn on a dime in Carousel Park. A few sunny days strung together and my wallet would be flush again and that meant a hotel. A few days - that's all I needed for my luck to turn.

This was not one of those days.

I see what you did there, Monday. I wish I could say I was amused.

A witch leaned against the driver's side door of the beat-up '69 orange and white Chevy pick-up that also made up my primary residence. But it wasn't just any old magic user. It was a dark witch. *The* dark witch - Jared Adams. He'd started hanging around Carousel Park the same time I started selling potions out of my truck.

My foster parents were normal. To say that limited my education on the witching world was an understatement. I didn't know much about being a witch but the one thing I knew for certain – Jared Adams wasn't to be trifled with.

He watched from the benches across the park while I performed readings and occasionally stopped to peruse my wares, scoffing at the ingredients listed on my handmade labels. He was a nuisance with a capital 'N'. It was a shame, too, because he was also nice to look at. Mysterious grey eyes emphasized by medium length, midnight hair that was tapered on the sides and an athletic build.

Good looks, great power, and an ego to match, Jared Adams was a trifecta of trouble.

On the upside, my house and I could drive as many miles away from him as my gas tank allowed – which at last check was somewhere around thirty-five. All I had to do was get past him.

"Ellie James." Jared pushed off the side of the pick-up and walked around to the back. "When are you going to take me up on my offer? It won't last forever."

Ignore him, Ellie. Just ignore him and he'll go away.

I fished my keys out of the front pocket of my jeans and unlocked the cap on the back of the truck. After shoving my sleeping bag off to the side, I tossed my back pack in the bed, locked everything back up, and made a dash to get behind the wheel and get the hell out of there.

Jared was lightning in motion. He whooshed by me and had the driver's door open before I made it around the side of the truck.

"You're a persistent son of a bitch, you know that?" I slid into the driver's seat and grabbed hold of the door to pull it closed. I needed something solid between me and Jared. "Why don't you find some other witch to play with and leave me alone?"

I called up my magic. The little that answered spit and sputtered its way to the surface. I knew it wouldn't be enough. I'd never have enough to deal with a witch like Jared but you work with what the Goddess gave you. I used it all to yank the truck door closed – only to have the door stay wide open.

Damn it all to hell.

One half of Jared's mouth upturned in a lopsided smile. "I could do this all day... but I won't." He released his magical hold on the door and it slammed against the frame, rocking the truck and me to one side. "What are you doing here, Ellie?"

"Making a living?" I pleaded to the Goddess as I turned the key in the ignition. *Please let it start. Please let it start.* The engine was misfiring but I didn't have the money to fix it. Not yet. I almost wept with joy when it roared to life without skipping a beat.

Jared leaned in to speak through the half open window. It was broken or I would have rolled it up and I mentally skyrocketed the repair to the top of a lengthy list. "You're not living. You're barely surviving."

"Yeah? Well, I'm not dead yet so don't count me out, Adams." The rearview mirror disagreed, however. The face reflected back at me was one I hardly recognized. Dark circles under hazel eyes, more pronounced cheekbones thanks to the pounds I shed after living so long on the street. In another life I was well rested and well fed.

Of course, that was before my family discovered I was a witch.

"I'm here to help, Ellie. All you have to do is ask." Jared removed himself from my window and winked out of sight.

I shifted the truck into drive and pulled away, praying he wasn't there the next morning.

• • • •

TUESDAY. MY FAVORITE day of the week. And that had everything to do with Pru. Not just because she brought me supplies but because she also brought me hope. Pru reminded me there was still good in the world. She believed in me, in my magic, and that it would lead to something amazing. She was five feet of positive energy, the total opposite of me and the only family I had left.

She was also uncharacteristically late.

I parked on the south side of the park, just like I did every Tuesday, and waited. Fifteen minutes past the hour, I started to worry. Thirty minutes, and I bordered on panic. It didn't matter that my fears were unfounded because I would know if Pru were in danger.

Somehow, I always knew.

Still, Pru prided herself on punctuality. *Something could have happened.* Worry plagued my mind but there were no real warning bells so I turned on the radio in an attempt to distract myself from the onslaught of worst-case scenarios running through my mind. The classic song about a New Orleans gambling house came on and my thoughts turned to my birth parents as the singer wailed about the troubles of his own family.

Was my mother the witch? My father? Both? This train of thought never led to anything good. There were always more questions and never any answers. This time proved no exception and was decidedly worse when my thoughts turned to Jared. He tried to lure me into training under him with promises of power and knowledge to harness my magic. I turned him down every time. But if he offered information of a different kind, like who I was and where I came from, would I still say no?

Salvation from myself and at least one question best left unanswered came in the form of a 1962 robin egg blue Volkswagon Bug. The distinct sound of a VW diesel engine drowned out my radio while the fumes filtered into the cab of my truck through the broken window. I'd never been so happy to choke on exhaust.

Pru.

After shutting off the truck, I hopped out of the cab and rushed to greet her before she had her door open. "You're late. Everything okay?"

"Mom's starting to suspect something." Pru stuffed her clutch purse into the glove box before getting out of the car and locking the door. She walked around to the front of the car and popped the trunk. Several bags stuffed with dry and canned goods were crammed inside the small storage compartment of the car. "This might be my last delivery for a while.... At least until I can throw her off the scent."

"Thanks, Pru." I rushed in for a hug. This was her biggest haul yet. I knew how much trouble she went to in order to get it. "This'll last me a month, if not more."

Her expression soured. "It's mostly fruit cups and granola bars. Oh, and a couple jars of peanut butter. But that's hardly a month's worth of supplies. Maybe if I—."

I grabbed two of the bags and headed toward my truck. "This is great Pru, seriously. Did you know peanut butter is a protein?" I jostled the bags to unlock the cap on my truck, almost spilling their contents when I caught Jared's reflection in the glass.

"Here, let me give you a hand." Pru came over and took one of the bags, unaware of the unwanted attention we'd drawn from across the street.

Jared never came around when Prudence visited me at the park. *Why now?* I tossed the bag into the back of the truck. When I turned around Jared was gone.

"Good thing there aren't any eggs in there." Pru shook her head in disapproval of the mess I'd made with the groceries. "Come on, let's get the rest loaded into your truck. I haven't had breakfast yet and I'm starving. Is the hot dog guy here?"

"Hot dogs aren't breakfast." My response was automatic. We had a similar exchange every Tuesday. Except this time, I made no move to help with the rest of the bags. I just stared at the empty spot where Jared stood seconds before.

"What's going on, Ellie? You seem edgy—more than normal, I mean." Pru rested a hand on my shoulder and gave a comforting squeeze. "You can tell me all about it over a dog with the works."

"No deal. I can't confide in someone while they're breathing hot sauerkraut breath in my face." I shook off the anxiousness from Jared's disappearing act. The last thing I needed was Pru looking into the dark witch – which she would, thoroughly, if I so much as mentioned his name.

The best thing for all involved – especially Pru – was to keep her as far from him as possible. Going through my sister was a sure-fire way for Jared to get to me.

And that wasn't going to happen.

Chapter Two

Another day. Another reading. I sipped the translucent brown water masquerading as coffee I'd bartered from Chuck, aka the hot dog guy, in exchange for a one card draw. He pulled the wheel of fortune – reversed. Change was coming and not for the better. He was disappointed in the reading. *That made two of us.* I was disappointed in the coffee. At least Chuck had a chance to do something about his future thanks to the cards. My coffee on the other hand... nothing could be done to improve that.

I waited for my first customer at the chess table under the sycamore tree away from the prying eyes of park goers out for their early morning exercise and sipped my drink. It was hot and melted away the morning chill, even if it tasted terrible.

A woman pushing a supped up stroller with oversized wheels jogged over to the table. Blonde hair pulled in a high and tight pony tail, make-up expertly applied, and workout attire that coordinated with the diaper bag tucked in the basket below a snoozing toddler. She looked like she had it together. Appearances could be deceiving.

So could the cards.

At least according to her. Another dissatisfied customer. If the readings kept going like the last two, I'd be run out of Carousel Park for sure. The jogger tossed around a few names like hustler and con artist – nothing I hadn't heard before – but she eventually handed over the money.

And by handed I mean tossed on the ground.

On hands and knees, I picked up the cash; spending extra time to make sure I hadn't missed a bill. I couldn't afford to lose a single dollar. Three weeks passed without a visit from Prudence. Supplies were low and my funds were lower. I hadn't realized how much I relied on her until she stopped coming around.

A pair of sensible black leather pumps stepped into view. They could have belonged to anyone if it weren't for the distinguishable scuff on the inside of the left shoe. Every left shoe she owned had that wear spot.

"Ellie."

The stern tone of her voice when she spoke my name jolted me to attention. I smacked my head against the concrete chess table on the way up. The thumping in my head marched to the same tune as my heart. It didn't matter that I no longer lived by her rules or under her roof. That woman still intimidated the hell out of me.

"Mrs. Harris." I stopped calling her mom the day she tossed me out on the street with nowhere to go and only the things I could carry. "What brings you to Carousel Park?"

Of course, I knew the answer.

She wouldn't step foot in the park, a place rumored to host magic users, if it didn't have something to do with her precious Prudence. I didn't blame my sister for the differences in our upbringing. Pru couldn't help that she was perfect. Just like she couldn't help that Mrs. Harris took notice of our differences the moment the Harris's welcomed her into their home. Whereas they'd grown to love Pru, they only tolerated my existence - until my magic manifested itself.

Barbara Harris drew a hard line at witchcraft.

"It's about Prudence." She fingered her pearl necklace. Something she did whenever she was upset – usually with me.

"Of course it is." I touched the spot on my head where it had connected with the table and sucked in a breath. Damn, that hurt. Fingertips slicked with blood, I wiped them clean on my jeans before I noticed the handkerchief Mrs. Harris held out to me.

That small sign of kindness raised all sorts of red flags.

"I need your help, Ellie." Her voice wavered as she closed the distance and ruined her crisp white monogramed handkerchief by pressing it against the cut on my scalp. Her hand trembled as she applied pressure. "You always were a walking disaster. Even as a child."

"Funny, I thought I heard you ask for my help." I jerked my head to one side and stepped out of her reach. "But then you opened your mouth again and the same old Barbara Harris came out."

"You must know how difficult this is for me. Coming here, *to you,* of all people." She looked at the handkerchief, lips pursed in distaste. "That'll never come out." She found a clean spot, wiped my blood off her hands, and tossed it in the green metal trash can.

I bit the inside of my cheek hard enough to draw blood to refrain from any snarky comments. It didn't matter if she was referring to my dirty witch blood or an ordinary stain. The sooner I found out why she needed – or more importantly why Pru – needed my help the better.

She never looked me in the eyes, not even when I lived in her house, but when she turned and held my gaze, the pain reflected there took my breath away.

"Where's Pru?"

"I don't know." There was the slightest quiver in her upper lip – the equivalent to an emotional outburst for the stoic Barbara Harris.

Something was wrong. Terribly wrong. And Prudence was involved. *I should have known. I used to know. So why not now?*

I'd feel it. As kids Pru and I knew when the other was hurt or in trouble. It didn't matter that we weren't twins or even related. We had a connection that went deeper than blood. Pru said it was my magic. I always said it was her heart. Whatever the reason, I would know.

"Why didn't you lead with that?" My hands were clenched into fists but I managed to cram them into my jeans pocket to avoid decking her. "We could have avoided the usual dance of insults and I could be out looking for her."

"'The police believe she's a runaway. Given our family's history, they...." Her hand instinctively went to her pearls again, counting each one like a devout Catholic would count their rosary. "We both know she'd never do that, if for no other reason than she'd never abandon you."

I knew how much that little admission cost her.

"I didn't run away. You tossed me out like garbage." After bundling my tarot deck in a scrap of burgundy velvet, I slipped it inside a black cotton draw string bag. I collected the rest of my stuff and closed up shop indefinitely, heading for my truck with Barbara on my heels.

"Yes, well, we couldn't exactly tell everyone that, now could we?" There she was, the side of Barbara reserved exclusively for me. "Then we'd have to explain what you truly are and nobody wants that."

"I know. What would the bridge club say? Or Harold's golf buddies? What a travesty really, but, you did your best, Barbara. You mustn't blame yourself."

I fished the keys out of my pocket, unlocked the driver's side door, and tossed my stuff on the bench seat. "How do they know she wasn't kidnapped or something? Running away is completely out of character for Prudence. She's nothing like me."

"There haven't been any ransom requests and... she left a note." Barbara reached into her purse and pulled out a piece of cream-colored card stock embossed with the family crest. The Harris's never discussed their wealth but they flaunted it at every opportunity. "Something about dreams. It's her handwriting but it doesn't sound like her."

"Can I see it?" I plucked the note from her hand without waiting for an answer.

Dreams are the key to what we refuse to see with our waking eye. I've gone to follow mine. Don't bother looking. - Pru

"It's her handwriting, yeah, but somebody forced her to write it. Dreams are the key to what we refuse to see...." I had no clue what any of it meant.

Pru always followed her dreams. She joked about how the best ideas came to her when she was asleep. She was whimsical but she also had a life plan by the time she was in fourth grade and never deviated from it. She wasn't the type to just up and run. Especially without telling me. It just wasn't in her nature.

"You think someone took her?" Barbara held out her hand expectantly, only dropping it back to her side when she realized I wasn't giving back the letter. "Keep that, if it will help."

"The ink here." I pointed to a spot where the ink swelled on the paper. "And here. She likes those gel pens. They bleed. It's like she hesitated while the point was still pressed against the paper. Maybe she was waiting for someone to tell her what to say."

"Harold said I should have come to you first. I hired a private investigator, spent thousands to get no more information than you just provided for free." Barbara reached into her designer bag and pulled out a matching envelope for the stationary.

A different kind of paper was stuffed inside.

"Seriously? You're a real piece of work, you know that, Barbara? Pru is my sister. You can cram that envelope—."

"How far do you expect to get in that run-down truck and the change in your pocket?" Barbara walked over and shoved the envelope against my chest. "Find her and bring her home, Ellie."

As much as it pained me to admit it, she was right. Between my slice of humble pie and swallowing my pride, I almost choked to death. I tucked the money in the waistband of my jeans and read the note again, tracing a finger along the flowery signature. Prudence had beautiful penmanship, feminine lines and curls, whereas my handwriting could be compared to a primate who recently learned she had opposable thumbs. A pang of guilt twisted my gut when I realized I already thought of her in the past tense.

Prudence wasn't dead. She was missing and I was going to find her.

Chapter Three

Barbara left the search to me and returned to the safety of her home in Brooke Heights, less than forty miles from Crescent Park but it might as well have been a world away. Its manicured lush green lawns and gated communities were a far cry from the city, bruised and battered from an economic exodus, I called home.

But Pru wasn't holed up in some cookie cutter mansion out in the Heights. Barbara wouldn't have lowered her standards and slummed it with a witch if she was. No, my sister was somewhere in the city. I just needed to find out where.

Tall order when you didn't have any clues to go on.

The clock started right after the Tuesday supply run three weeks earlier. The police started from the last place the Harris's had seen her, but that wasn't the last place she'd been seen. I decided to see what the Harris family fortune could get me and greased a few palms. Pru had a few haunts between Crescent Park and the guest house on the Harris estate that she'd taken over when she started college.

Four Benjamins and three security tapes later, I got a hit—Gaea's Garden, an herbalist and natural market on the Gaston city line. Prudence swore by their soy candles and essential oils. I wouldn't know – bath bombs weren't my thing. Truck stops and KOAs don't have soaker tubs and even if they did, aromatherapy wasn't on my list of necessities.

The young woman working behind the counter greeted me with a smile when I walked in. "Welcome to Gaea's. Can I help you find anything?"

"Funny you should ask." The security sensor beeped again as the door closed behind me. "I'm trying to find my sister."

"That's not really our area of expertise. I mean, we have divination candles and incense. They're supposed to help with—." One look at the stone-cold expression on my face cut her sales pitch short. "Sorry. I just started here and I have zero retail experience. Or customer service experience, to be honest. I'm not really sure how I got this job in the first place."

"Maybe you could just look at a couple of pictures and tell me if you've seen her in here, okay?" I pulled my phone out of my back pocket and opened the gallery.

Pru was the first photo. She had mustard and relish on both sides of her mouth, her cheeks packed full of the hot dog she ate for lunch. Her arms were raised in triumph after challenging me to a race to see who could finish first.

I let her win.

The clerk came over to look at the picture. "She's your sister? You guys don't look anything alike."

"We're adopted." *Well, one of us was.* "Have you seen her?"

"Yeah, sure. She was here the other day." She tapped her pointer finger against her chin. "Tuesday. I remember because she was a big ticket and used a bunch of those Visa gift cards."

"You remember what she bought?" *Gift cards? Prudence had credit cards and a spending allowance.*

"Um, yeah, it sounded Italian." The girl's bleach blonde ponytail swung wildly as she walked with purpose back behind the counter. "It was Bella something. I can look it up if you want."

"Belladonna." I hid my surprise over the revelation Pru wasn't there purchasing bath bombs or incense.

The clerk snapped her fingers. "That's it. Belladonna."

I grabbed a business card from the clear plastic holder on the counter and wrote my cell number on the back. "If you see her or think of anything else, call this number."

She opened the register, lifted the cash drawer, and slid the card underneath for safe keeping. I thanked her for her time and left the shop with more questions than answers.

There were two reasons for purchasing belladonna – a sleeping draft or poisoning someone. She bought enough to tranquilize an elephant. Or poison half a dozen people.

What are you up to, Pru?

After that the trail went cold. She drove out of Gaston and, as far as I could tell, headed home. I'd hit a dead end. With no other leads, I drove back to Crescent Park. After stopping at the gas station on West Street to refuel, I pulled the truck into my usual spot. The truck wasn't the only one with an empty tank. After chasing down any lead I could find, I was running on fumes so I splurged on a couple donuts and a large coffee.

My brain needed sugar and, well, the rest of me needed the caffeine.

Lost in my thoughts about Pru's last visit to the park, I almost choked on my cruller when Jared rapped a knuckle on my window. I swallowed and said, "Please go away."

"Things must be looking up. Coffee *and* donuts." Jared leaned against the side of the truck.

"I said please." I set my coffee on the dash and licked donut glaze off my fingertips.

"I noticed." He gave me a half smile and I wasn't sure who I hated more – Jared or my hormones. "Where's your friend? The one with the pretty black braids?"

The seemingly innocuous question hit me like a shot of adrenaline to the heart. I was out of the truck and in his face before I even realized what I was doing. "What do you know about my sister?"

"Ellie." Jared must have seen something feral in my eyes because his hands were raised as if he was being held at gun point. "You need to calm down or one of us is going to get hurt. And while I find you intriguing, if I have to choose, it's not going to be me."

"Calm down? My sister is missing and then you show up, with all your dark magic swirling around you, asking about her and you want me to calm down?" My heart raced faster than a jackrabbit, pumping blood and magic through my veins.

Too much magic.

No, no, no. Not again. Memories of the day I was unintentionally ousted out of the metaphorical broom closet resurfaced. It was a Thursday. That much I remember—kind of hard to forget when it's your eighteenth birthday—but for the life of me I couldn't remember the specific reason I'd drawn Barbara's ire. Not that it mattered; she had dozens of reasons, none of them rational. No, what mattered was I lost control of my temper and that's when my magic manifested itself.

Apparently, I was a late bloomer.

My hair stood on end as static energy charged the air. Tiny shards of glass rained down when the recessed lights in the ceiling exploded. Small flames burst from the outlets in the wall. Barbara screamed. I blacked out. My bags were packed when I woke up. After multiple trips to the library and countless Google searches, Pru and I figured out I was a witch. Stress was a trigger and something I tried hard to avoid.

Jared plus stress? That was a disaster waiting to happen.

Inhale, exhale. Inhale, exhale. I closed my eyes and counted to ten. And then counted again but I couldn't dispel the energy. It hurt. A lot. I bit my lip hard enough to draw blood to hold back the cries of pain but a small whimper escaped. Jared rested a hand on my shoulder, whispered something in a language I didn't understand, and just like—ha-ha—magic the pain went away. So did all the pent-up energy. My legs gave out and my knees hit the pavement, my teeth clacking together on impact. I wiped the sweat from my brow and pushed the unruly strands of hair out of my face.

"You should really take me up on my offer, Ellie. There's more to being a witch than reading cards. You're going to kill yourself if you don't at least learn the basics." Jared looked at me with renewed interest but left me sitting on the pavement. He stepped around the open driver's door and grabbed my coffee and donuts off the dash. "Here, you need the sugar. Something with electrolytes would be better but I guess the coffee will have to do."

"Thanks." I managed a meek smile. "Listen, I appreciate what you just did, but I'm not into...." I waved my hand up and down. "This."

"You just gestured to all of me." He wore a confident smile, like he knew I would in fact be into some of him. "Oh, you mean my magic? Afraid to come to the dark side, Ellie?"

I washed down a mouthful of donut with cold coffee. "No."

That was a lie. He knew it and I knew it. Truth be told, I was terrified.

"I tell you what, I'll make you a deal. An offer you can't refuse." Jared leaned back against my truck, arms folded across his chest. "You quit shuffling cards in the park and come work for me. The pay sucks but the continuing education program is outstanding."

"If you do say so yourself." I polished off the last cruller and drained the coffee cup dry. A headache was blossoming behind my right eye, no doubt an allergic reaction to so much time spent with Jared. I needed a bottle of water and a couple of aspirin. "So, you get what you want and I get? What exactly?"

"I'll help you find your sister."

And there it was. The one carrot Jared could dangle in front of my face that I was sure to follow.

"Deal." I held out my hand, ready to shake on it.

"I'm going to need something more than a handshake." Jared reached out and caressed my chestnut tresses.

The slight wobble in my knees had nothing to do with the way he ran his fingers through my hair. It was residual magic. *Yeah, that's it, residual magic.*

"Ouch. That hurt, Jared. What the hell." Pulled from my moment of weakness swooning over Jared Adams, I rubbed the sore spot on my scalp where he'd yanked out a lock of hair.

"Now we have a deal." He knotted the strands of hair and slipped them into his pocket. "Rest up, James. You're going to need it. My shop, tonight. Nine o'clock. Don't be late."

• • • •

CAULDRON CRAFTS SAT on the corner of Carrick and Rogers. I sat in my truck in a parking space out front. Jared knew I was there. My pick-up backfired when I shifted to park, announcing my presence to everyone within a three-block radius.

"You can do this, Ellie. You have to do this." It was the fourth pep talk I'd given myself but my hands still gripped the steering wheel.

I knew what I had to do. I just had a hard time doing it. Magic – when I managed to get it to work – felt amazing. Almost too amazing. From what I'd heard, black magic felt even more so. It's how witches get hooked and their gift corrupted. I barely had a gift. It would be a shame to corrupt what little magic I had.

Jared watched me from behind the storefront window as he pulled the chain dangling from the neon OPEN sign. The bright blue light blinked out but not before a smirk settled across his lips as he, no doubt, took pleasure in my personal battle to get out of the truck. He pulled something from the small pocket on his button-down shirt. I watched him twirl it around his finger twice before I realized what it was – and the real reason for the smile on his face.

I reached across the seat, grabbed my backpack and hopped out of the truck before Jared could force me to do it. With a few strands of my hair, I'd be a marionette on a string. There were limitations, of course; you couldn't force someone to commit murder or to give themselves to you – unless they wanted to. There are lines people won't cross even under a compulsion spell. When forced, the brain revolts and the end result is messy.

But forcing me to get out of my truck and into his shop? Easy.

Jared held open the door as I rushed inside. "Afraid someone will see you?"

"No." I lied.

He wasn't convinced. Neither was I. Black magic was bad for business and business in Crescent Park was slow enough as it was. People came around to dabble in their fortunes or for some herbs to make their arthritis better, not real magic. Hanging out with Jared was a sure-fire way to lose what little clientele I had.

It was also the only way I could find Pru.

I'd made a deal with the devil. I always kept my word and managed to walk away clean. But this time I wasn't so sure.

Chapter Four

Cauldron Crafts was nothing like I had expected. Bookshelves lined the walls and four large retail displays filled the center of the store. Herbs, bone shards, and other ingredients for all your spelling needs hung from pegs in individually wrapped plastic packages, each labeled and stocked according to their desired purpose. It was neat, organized, and clean enough to eat off the floors. If his wares weren't of the magical variety, his shop could have passed for any other store in Gaston City.

"Ellie James." Jared leaned against the glass display case which doubled as a counter top. He smiled like the cat that ate the canary, like he knew something I didn't. Goddess help him if it was about my sister. "You know, I was starting to doubt my powers of persuasion. I didn't think I'd ever see you walk into my store."

"I hate to burst your bubble there but your powers of persuasion let you down. I'm here because of Prudence." I crossed my arms over my chest and leaned a hip against the display case opposite him. Feigning confidence we both knew I didn't have, I asked the question burning a hole in my gut since I pulled up. "Now that I'm here, how exactly do you propose to help me find her?"

He clapped his hands together. "I love the enthusiasm, James. I really do. Step into my office." He pushed open the hip-high swinging door in the end of the counter which separated staff from patron.

The cautionary tale of the spider and fly came to mind as I followed him through a narrow doorway hidden behind a sun-bleached velvet curtain into the back of the store. My pulse quickened and my palms began to sweat as my imagination ran wild with possibilities of what awaited me behind the curtain – a blood coven intent on bringing me into the fold, an altar for a sacrifice with me as the lamb, or a portal to hell. Countless hours of my youth spent watching B-horror movies told me I was making a fatal mistake following Jared away from prying eyes.

This is where the damsel dies. Every time.

Once again, Jared surprised me. I was not prepared for the level of normalcy inside the walls of his establishment. His storeroom wasn't stocked with supplies or torture devices of my imagination. No, it was a workshop every witch dreamed of owning. Copper spelling pots hung from culinary racks fastened into the ceiling. Herbs hung upside down from drying racks. Wooden countertops lined the room with a large island in the center, complete with a drop-down gas range.

Color me green with envy.

My shoddy potions and gris-gris bags might actually be worth something if I had a space like his. Without waiting for an invitation, I gave myself the grand tour of his workspace, stopping to peruse the jars lined neatly along the wall on the far-left countertop. Chills ran down my spine when I saw both wet and dry specimens inside the sealed glass containers. Everything I expected and feared I would find inside a black magic shop was there in plain view. Jared didn't try to hide who or what he was.

Eager to get his help and get the hell out of there, I turned my attention away from his spelling supplies and back to where it should have been – with Pru. "So, my sister—what do you need to find her?"

"I'm not going to find her, Ellie. You are. Go stand over there." Jared pointed to the center of the room and tossed a piece of chalk he grabbed off the counter in my direction.

I was supposed to catch it. I missed. Shards of broken chalk littered the floor.

A lopsided grin softened his features as he raked a hand through his hair. "It's just magnetic chalk. It won't bite."

"I know that. You caught me off guard." That wasn't even a half truth and he knew it as well as I did. The truth? I didn't trust Jared. It didn't matter what he threw at me, I wasn't going to catch it.

He picked up a new piece of chalk, tucked it in the pocket of his shirt and walked over to where I was standing. He swept the remnants of the first piece out of the way with his foot, took me by the hand and led – or dragged, depending on who you asked – me to the center of the room.

"Draw a circle." He offered me the new piece of chalk. "Honestly, Ellie. It's rudimentary stuff. I use this with my younger students to help them focus."

"People let you teach their kids?" My eyes widened to the size of silver dollars when I realized I said that out loud.

He was gracious enough to laugh off the slight. "Contrary to popular belief, black magic isn't about sacrificing children. You can blame the Grimm brothers for starting that rumor."

There was a slight tremble in my hand as I took the chalk. After a deep breath, I gauged the size of the circle I wanted. "You're not going to be in it, right?" When he shook his head, I waved him back a few steps. "Okay, give me some room."

With the tip of the chalk pressed against the concrete floor, I started on my right and made one complete rotation. I stood up to admire my work. Geometrically speaking, calling my drawing a circle was a stretch of the imagination. It was closer to an oval with wobbly edges.

Pru was in trouble and I was already failing Witching 101. Relying on magic – my magic – was a mistake.

Jared recognized the disappointment on my face and offered a few words of encouragement. "It's fine, Ellie. It doesn't have to be perfect, just round... Or, mostly round." One corner of his mouth crooked up in a smile as he winked at me. "Connected is really the key, as long as there are no breaks in the circle, you're fine."

I slipped the chalk in my pocket and wiped my hands on the front of my jeans, leaving white trails on my thighs. "Now what?"

"Close your eyes." Jared returned my stare with a frustrated glare. "A little trust would be nice. I haven't given you a reason not to."

Not yet anyway. Trust and faith went out the window when I went out on the street. The only exception was Pru. She was the reason I stood inside a wonky circle in the middle of Jared's workspace so I forced myself to close my eyes. "Now what?"

"I want you to concentrate and open your third eye." I heard him move to the edge of the circle in front of me, the sweet smell of peppermint on his breath wafting toward me a few seconds later.

"My third eye is legally blind, so...." I opened my eyes and shrugged. I was only half joking.

"Focus." Jared snapped. "If you want to find your sister—."

"It's hard to focus on anything other than what a monumental waste of time this is. I'm going to find Prudence with or without my busted magic." Anger and frustration over my ineptitude sparked a flare up of energy.

The overhead lights flickered before exploding. Tiny pieces of glass rained down, blanketing the floor like winter frost. Jared rushed to the counter on the left, grabbed a spelling pot off the hot plate, and tossed its contents at me. My arms instinctively went up to block my face from scalding water as I stepped backward and broke the circle.

"Are you crazy?" I shouted, only slightly relieved as tepid – not boiling - salt water doused me from head to toe.

"If by 'crazy' you mean wanting to stay alive, then yeah, I'm crazy." The spelling pot clattered against the floor when Jared dropped it. Arms akimbo with his palms facing out, he dipped his chin toward his chest. He looked at me through half lidded eyes as he muttered something that sounded a lot like Latin, but not.

He cast a spell.

I backed up, smearing what remained of the chalk circle. "Jared? What are you doing?" My voice cracked, exposing the fear gripping my heart.

His magic answered for him. A warm blast of air hit me. Within seconds, my clothes and hair were dry.

"Not all the spells I know are dark magic, Ellie." Jared bent down and picked up the pot, setting it back on the counter.

"Well, how was I supposed to…." I stopped the defensive quip mid-stream. As much as it physically pained me to admit it, he was right. "I'm sorry. I shouldn't have assumed the worst."

"You have a tendency to do that where I'm concerned." Jared wasn't wrong but I had the decency to look chagrined when he said it.

I raked my fingers through my hair as I choked on another apology, expecting them to snag in tangles at the end. When they didn't, I eyed Jared with suspicion. A mirror hung from two hooks beneath a shelf above the counter. Nudging past Jared, I used the witch's glass to check my reflection.

"You dried my clothes *and* gave me the best blowout of my life."

"I feel like there's a joke there but I'll let it slide." Jared's playful wink matched his smile. He leaned in and my heart skipped a beat – not from fear but something else. The intoxicating smell of magic still swirled around him as he reached around me. It was a heady mix of all the elements—a camp fire in the fall, crisp winter air before the first snowfall, freshly tilled soil ripe for planting in the spring and the whiff of ozone before the sky is electrified in a summer storm. It was intoxicating and I couldn't resist the urge to breath him in. He broke the spell he'd unwittingly spun by shoving an old tattered tome in my hands. "Here, when we're not working on your magic or looking for Prudence, I want you studying this."

"You're a lot different than I imagined." Careful not to stress the weakened spine, I flipped the worn book open to the table of contents.

"So, you *have* been thinking about me." Jared's smile widened. "I knew it."

"Your ego is big enough. I'm not feeding it." I traced a handwritten note on the page with my finger. Scrawled in the margins beside chapter headings were the words "Property of Jared Adams. If found, please return – or else." *Now THAT is the Jared I imagined.*

"I don't suppose you have something of your sister's—." Jared's phone rang. He pulled his cell from his pocket and looked at the number. "I have to take this."

I started to protest about the personal belongings and their no doubt intended uses in black magic but he cupped the phone in his hand and whispered, "Hold on," before going back to his argument over fake artifacts with an apparently unhappy customer. It sounded like everything was not on the up and up at Cauldron Crafts.

Color me surprised.

"We're not summoning Prudence like she's some sort of demon." I pushed off the counter, grabbed my messenger bag off the floor, and slung it over my shoulder. "This is a waste of time. I'll see you around, Adams."

I made it as far as the front door before Jared evoked the charm he made from my hair. Yet another reason I wouldn't give him Pru's, even if I had had some.

"We made a deal, Ellie." He mumbled something in the same strange language as before and immediately my body ignored all commands from my brain and moved on its own accord – well, technically Jared's, stopping me in my tracks. The spell also rendered me speechless – there's a first time for everything – but if looks could kill, he'd be dead on the floor.

"You need my help as much as Prudence needs yours." Something in his voice, a hint of desperation so small I almost missed it, said he needed my help, too.

Jared Adam had ulterior motives. Hell, his ulterior motives had ulterior motives. If I wanted to survive my partnership with Jared and find my sister, I needed to uncover them.

And fast.

Chapter Five

"If I let you go, do you promise to behave and stick to our agreement?" Jared dialed back the spell enough for me to move my mouth but not my limbs.

Smart man.

A slew of expletives pronounced my struggle against the charm. Every cell in my body burned as I battled to regain control of my arms and legs. My muscles knotted into pretzels, torn between Jared's charm and my sheer determination. My clothes clung to the fine dew of sweat coating my body. Seconds dragged into minutes of excruciating pain before I lost the battle of magic and wills against Jared.

"Fine." I ground out between clenched teeth. "I'll behave."

Jared snapped his fingers and I collapsed into a heap on the floor. "When you're ready, meet me in the back. We'll pick up where we left off."

"We're not summoning my sister." I panted as a wave of exhaustion hit me.

"There you go again. Assuming the worst." Jared left me on the floor and went in the back room.

"I deserved that." I muttered to myself. Still too tired to move from my spot on the cold tile floor, sleep claimed me.

It was anything but restful. Prudence ran laps in the recesses of my subconscious, calling out for help. Calling my name. I tried to catch up to her, to let her know I was looking for her, but I couldn't gain any ground. The harder I ran, the further away she was. I woke in a fit with her name on my lips and Jared kneeling over me.

"We'll find her, Ellie." He brushed a wayward strand of hair out of my face. "We'll find your sister. Here, drink this."

My mouth felt like the Sahara. My throat was raw enough from screaming Prudence's name that I didn't question what was in the cup Jared handed me. That was a mistake. Bitter and acidic, the tonic triggered every gag reflex I had but I managed to force it down. It hit my stomach with the same vengeance, threatening to come back up. I belched in a very unladylike fashion. I clamped a hand over my mouth and swallowed hard, praying it didn't find its way out my nose. Between failing at my first magical test, losing to Jared's charm, and collapsing on the floor, my pride had taken enough hits. I didn't need to add projectile vomiting to my list of humiliating events. "What was in that?"

Jared grimaced. "Sometimes things get worse before they get better. That tonic, for example. You'll feel sick as a dog for a couple minutes but if you get past the nausea without actually throwing up, you'll feel better."

I managed a thumbs up with the hand that wasn't covering my mouth.

"Come on." Jared hooked his arms under mine and hoisted me up off the floor. He held on, to ensure my legs were steady as we walked to the back of the store.

The spring was back in my step before we were in his workshop. Jared had an annoying habit of being right. He also had an annoying habit of being accidentally helpful and charming. I untangled myself from his side and stood on my own two feet before I got caught up in his intoxicating scent again.

"Take a look at chapter three." Jared held out the tattered tome I'd tossed on the counter when I'd attempted to bail on our agreement.

Focusing Objects

Focus is the key to any spell. Concentrating on the target while maintaining control over one's magic can be difficult for the rudimentary witch. A focus object can be a useful tool until the student advances to more complicated crafting. Depending on the desired results, personal items or physical totems such as four-leaf clovers for luck or a coin for wealth can be very effective.

The heaping slice of humble pie I was about to serve myself was harder to swallow than Jared's tonic.

"So, you don't want to summon Prudence?" I asked, an apologetic smile plastered on my face.

"It might make things easier if were possible but it's not." Jared patted his hand against his pocket where the charm binding my free will to his resided. "Unless you have one of these." Before I could utter an *aha*!, he held up his hands. "Kidding, I'm kidding. You can only summon demons."

I did a quick mental inventory of everything in my truck. "I don't have anything of Pru's. I could call Barbara. She might be—."

"Absolutely not." Jared's voice iced over, matching look in his eyes at the mention of my former foster mother. "You're only making one call to that woman and that's when we find Prudence."

"Have you met my foster mother?" I couldn't imagine a scenario where their paths would have crossed but he seemed to share in my dislike of her.

"No, and I don't need to. Her hate and fear put you on the street. A household of bigots, high on the hill." He shook his head. "Prudence excluded, of course. You should count yourself lucky to be rid of them."

"I do." And I meant it, but that didn't make being shunned hurt any less. I cleared my throat and wiped away the tear threatening to slip out from the corner of my eye. "Without a focus object, where does that leave us?"

"Well, it doesn't make things any easier, but I've got a few spells up my sleeves." He ran his fingers through his cropped hair. "You burned through enough of the Harris's Benjamins. Let's see what it got you."

I shook my head. "Not a thing. Unless a receipt for bath-bombs and belladonna is helpful."

"Did Prudence have trouble sleeping?"

"Can you please stop referring to her in past tense?" Dust plumed from the worn pages as I slammed the book shut. "She's alive. I know it."

"I just meant in the past." Jared's words and his hands held up in a placating gesture said he believed me – Pru was still alive – but his eyes told another story. Jared promised we'd find my sister. He just didn't promise what condition we'd find her in.

I'd know if she were dead.

Like I should have known from the start? Doubt crept in but I pushed it back. I didn't sense she was in trouble. I couldn't change that but... I would sense it if she were dead. *I would.*

"Hey." Jared snapped his fingers. "Hello? Earth to Ellie."

"Sorry." I pulled myself back from my fritzy magic and lack of warnings and thought about what he asked me. "No, no insomnia or anything like that. In fact...." I paused, thinking back on all the years we shared a room. "She slept like the dead. She always remembered her dreams when she woke up and kept a journal in the top drawer of the nightstand by her bed. I never remembered mine. I always envied her that when we were growing up."

Jared went from piqued to captivated. "Belladonna can intensify visions."

"She has vivid dreams. Not visions." I tapped him on the shoulder when he brushed off my response. "Are you listening?"

"I'm totally listening." Except he wasn't. He ransacked the shelves, knocking two large wooden stirring spoons from their hooks on the chef's rack overhead in the process. "Visions."

"That is the exact opposite of what I said." I grabbed hold of one of his hands to slow the fury of flying books, only to jump back three steps when he exclaimed, "Found it!"

"Here, look at this." Jared set down another written relic in worse condition than the last. What pages weren't missing were blackened on the edges, the cover half-burnt. But through the cracked and crisp exterior, the original silver embossing was still legible.

Dreamwalkers.

"What does this have to do with Prudence?" I asked, completely confused with the direction our conversation was headed.

"Everything." He carefully opened the book and turned to one of the few intact pages, tapping a finger by the title. "Belladonna."

"That's fascinating, really. Except Prudence isn't a dreamwalker. She's just every day ordinary Prudence." I cringed at my choice of words. Prudence didn't need magic to be magical and she was anything but ordinary. But she wasn't a witch or a dreamwalker.

Jared reached into his pocket and pulled out the charm whose main ingredient was a lock of my hair and set it on the countertop between us. "I'm willing to bet she is."

"That's a bold move." The charm mocked me from its place on the counter. He wouldn't risk losing a powerful trinket if he wasn't confident in his assumption.

"If I'm wrong, I destroy the charm." He hesitated, waiting to see if I'd prompt him for the other half of the wager. After a moment, he continued. "If I'm right, you stay on another month without it."

"So either way the charm's gone?" I'll admit, I was tempted by the offer.

Trust Jared not to abuse the charm while we searched for Pru when I hadn't uncovered his ulterior motives? Or keep working with him beyond our initial agreement and keep my free will?

Jared nodded. "No charms. I win, you stay four more weeks. You win, I destroy the charm and you can walk out of here. If you still want to."

His confidence, annoying as it was, wasn't misplaced. He knew I wasn't walking out of there with or without the charm in effect. Pru was the reason I agreed to his "help" in the first place. She was still out there somewhere. Until I found her, I was stuck with him.

But Jared wasn't the only confident one.

"Okay, it's a bet." I held out my hand.

Jared clasped his hand around mine and sealed the deal with an old-fashioned and magic-free handshake. "I don't suppose you still have a key to the Harris estate?"

"If I did, Barbara would have changed the locks. Why?" My stomach churned in anticipation of his answer.

"Give Babs a call. Tell her we'll be stopping by." He checked his watch. "And to put some coffee on."

"First of all, 'Babs' doesn't put coffee on. Rosaria does." My mouth watered with the memory of her café au lait. Nothing compared. "And second, fifteen minutes ago we weren't asking Barbara for help. Now we are?"

"We need to get into Pru's room." Jared grabbed a back pack and started filling it with various charms- some more innocuous than others- and the charred book on dreamwalkers.

I gestured at him. "All this power and we can't even bypass the front door." I dreaded the call. For numerous reasons but mainly because I had zero updates on Prudence.

"Bemoaning the limitations of our magical options doesn't change anything. It's witchcraft, not Star Fleet. We can't beam ourselves up. Make the call, Ellie." He tapped his wrist where a watch face would rest if he actually wore one.

Tick-tock.

The clock was ticking. The first forty-eight hours were crucial to any investigation. I wasn't a detective and that critical mark passed long before I knew Prudence was missing. My playbook consisted of knowledge gained from an earlier obsession with cold case documentaries and relying on Jared for magical support.

In other words, things weren't looking good.

I pulled my phone out of my jeans pocket and dialed the Harris's number from memory.

"You found her. Harold, it's Ellie." Sounds of Barbara's attempt to wake her husband came over the line. "She found Prudence."

Barbara's ability to manage happiness and disappointment at the same time never ceased to amaze me.

I thought I'd gotten used to the way she said my name with disdain, even in casual conversation, but it still stung. The phantom pains of old wounds were replaced with new and deeper ones when I corrected her.

"Barbara." I waited a breath for her to finish proclaiming the *good news* to interrupt her again. "Barbara. I haven't found her. It's like she vanished between Gaea's Garden and the gate to your estate."

"Dare I even ask the reason for this phone call? At... what time *is* it?" She paused, most likely to check the clock on her nightstand. "Three in the morning. Let me guess. You need more money. I should have known better. Your *abilities* haven't done you any good before now. I was a fool to expect—."

"Shut. Up." The phone creaked under the pressure of my grip as I struggled to reign in my temper. Old arguments threatened to raise their ugly heads but I refused to take the bait. "I need to see Pru's room."

"Here? Is that really necessary?" Barbara sounded stricken, as if the idea of a witch in her house made her physically ill.

Wait until she realized it wasn't one witch but two. I admit, I perked up bit over her discomfort. "Does she have a room somewhere else? Yes, *there.*" I checked my attitude and tried again. "I won't stay long. Half an hour, just long enough to look for some sort of clue."

"The police have searched her room and didn't...." The fight left her with one heavy exhale. "Pull around to the back of the house and use the service entrance."

She hung up before I could say thank you, which was a testament to how much Pru's disappearance had taken out of her. Normally she wouldn't miss an opportunity to hear me choke on my gratitude.

"That went well." I almost pulled a muscle with my eye roll.

Jared ruffled through a few jars, grabbed a pack of assorted candles, what looked like incense and a sachet of herbs, and shoved all the items in his backpack before tossing me mine. I caught it with my chest and a resounding oompf.

A buzzer sounded and the monitor mounted to the wall flickered to life, showing a petite woman wrapped in a fur stole, sandwiched between two men in tailored suits. The woman motioned to the doorbell and the man on her right obliged. The buzzer sounded again.

"I'll drive." Jared fished a set of keys out of the front pocket of his jeans.

"Another unhappy customer?"

"We should go." Jared grabbed my hand and pulled me in the direction of the back door. "Like now."

"Jared." My attention was fixed on the monitor even as he tugged on my arm. "How did she do that?"

With a touch of her finger the woman dropped all three locks on the front door of Cauldron Crafts. The tempered glass door swung open. She waited for her guards to enter before crossing the threshold. Her gaze flicked to the camera. The deviant look in her eyes combined with the wicked grin said all I needed to know about the mystery woman in Jared's store. She was dangerous with a capital D. Small electrical charges crackled between her palms just before the monitor blinked out.

Magic.

"I'll explain it later. Ellie, come on." Jared swiped at the air with his left hand. The emergency exit obeyed his command and swung open without tripping the alarm.

"She's a witch?"

"Most of my customers are. Will you come on?" Jared shoved me through the door, yanking it shut as soon as my feet hit the parking lot. He pulled a Sharpie from his back pocket and scribbled half a dozen symbols on the metal door.

"Will that stop them?" I hitched my backpack higher on my shoulders, clutching the straps as if they'd provide some layer of added security.

"It'll buy us a few minutes." Jared unhooked a full face helmet from beneath the back seat of a blue and white race bike and tossed it at me. "That's all we need."

"You want me to get on the back of that?" My heart flip-flopped before seizing in fear. "I've never ridden before."

"You're welcome to stay here and talk things out with Helene." Jared pulled his helmet on and turned the engine. The bike rumbled to life.

What would Helene and I have to talk about? Her beef was with Jared. Not me. Against my better judgment, I hopped on the back of his bike and cinched my arms around his waist like a python coiling around its prey.

For once, visiting the Harris estate seemed like the lesser of two evils.

Still, a sense of dread weighed on my mind. I felt like I made a deal with the devil. Black magic, shady business practices, and powerful, pissed off customers? I prayed to the Goddess I was right about Prudence.

I wasn't sure I'd survive four weeks with Jared Adams if I was wrong.

Chapter Six

W e crossed the Gaston City line in record time. Rundown buildings and green grass blurred together as Jared drove us into Brooke Heights at speeds which should have broken the sound barrier. Fortunately for him, we left my stomach somewhere near the carousel as we blazed through Crescent Park, so he was spared me projectile vomiting when we stopped at the gate to the Harris estate.

I unlocked my frozen fingers from around Jared's waist, flipped up the visor on my helmet, and pressed the button on the intercom.

"Ellie James and Jared Adams to see Mrs. Barbara Harris. Please." I said, between chattering teeth.

I hated the formality. The illusion of perfection within the walls of the Harris household had suffocated me when I was growing up.

Goddess please let me get in, get the journals, and get out unscathed. Oh, and be right about Pru. I added the fourth request at the last second, almost forgetting that key point as I sent up my prayer to the Goddess. *Please let me be right about Prudence.*

The gate swung open without a response from anyone inside the house. Jared drove up the long drive at a respectable speed and pulled around back as instructed. I couldn't get off the bike fast enough. I staggered to the servant's entrance with all the grace and elegance of a newborn calf and gripped one of the porch columns until I regained my stability, only then ringing the bell.

"Why couldn't we take my truck?" I asked, still leaning on the column for support. "It has heat." *Most of the time.*

Jared responded with halfhearted laughter. "If we took your truck we'd be talking to Helene and her goons right now instead of looking for your sister."

"Yeah, umm.... About Helene—."

A member of the Harris's staff, one I didn't recognize, opened the door wearing crisp white pajamas and a matching robe with the Harris crest emblazoned on the chest pocket. He motioned for us to come inside before I could ask Jared if there would be more run ins and narrow escapes in the immediate future. "Miss James. This way, please."

We followed the butler inside, through the staff quarters, and up a set of stairs that led to the kitchen. From there we were escorted to the French doors which led out to the veranda. The guest house, where Prudence stayed, was down a set of concrete steps, past the Olympic sized swimming pool and roughly an eighth of a mile walk across sprawling grass kept green year long by Hector the gardener.

If I didn't know better, I'd swear he used magic.

"You grew up here?" Jared looked over his shoulder at the massive stone house looming over us on the hill then back to me, shaking his head in disbelief.

"It was my childhood and I hardly believe it." I offered a meek smile and tried to not to think about my years of being the Harris's black sheep – even before they discovered what I was.

Still, it hadn't been all bad.

Hector had let me drive the tractor and help tend the Victorian herb garden. My limited knowledge of herbal medicine came from lessons over a bag of fertilizer and a pair of pruning shears. If it wasn't for Hector, the gris-gris bags I sold out of the back of my truck in Crescent Park would be worthless. Rosaria slipped me empanadas from her private stash after school and, of course, there was Prudence. From playmate to confidant, she'd always had my back. We were inseparable.

Until Barbara tossed me out.

A golf cart waited for us at the bottom of the steps with the key still in the ignition. Bumper stickers from local bands plastered the back of the motorized cart and there was a miniature vanity plate that said 'Pru' attached to the bumper.

"So this is how the other half lives?" Jared laughed. "I often wondered if it was true."

"Please, like you're suffering in poverty." I rolled my eyes. "You have a business, albeit it a shady one. Still, it's a regular income. You have a roof over your head, food whenever you want it, a car, a motorcycle... hot water."

Things I was forced to give up.

I left the golf cart and Jared where they were and headed for the guest house. Dew coating the grass soaked through the canvas of my All-Stars and into my socks before dampening the hem of my jeans. The sun wouldn't crest the horizon for a few more hours. The freezing bike ride combined with the breeze whipping across the open yard and wet shoes set a chill deep in my bones. Warmth—and with any luck clues to Pru's whereabouts—awaited inside the guest house. I flipped up the collar of my jacket, shoved my hands in my pockets, and quickened my pace.

Jared sprinted to catch up, his boots tromping Hector's perfectly trimmed grass. "Sorry, I can be an ass some times."

"I've noticed." Not in a particularly forgiving mood, I shrugged off his apology. The wet grass wasn't the only thing dampening my mood. Being home again had me on edge. We walked the rest of the way in silence.

As expected, the door to the guest house was unlocked. The gate and security systems in place on the property gave a false sense of security. Pru's disappearance was proof positive.

Strings of twinkle lights illuminated the ceiling, resembling a clear summer sky full of stars. Billowy tulle draped around the headboard, piles of throw pillows and an oversized duvet completing the fairy princess décor. Everything was soft, feminine, pink, and totally Prudence.

"She's in college, right?" Jared picked up a throw pillow from the floor and tossed it into the pile on the bed.

"When she was in first grade, Pru's teacher told her she could be what ever she wanted to be. She took that message to heart." I stepped around him to reach the nightstand where I assumed Pru kept her dream diaries.

"And she wanted to be a princess?" Jared asked, apparently still dumfounded by my sister's taste in decorating.

"We're witches. You're convinced she's some sort of dream weaver. At this point, anything is possible. So, why not a fairy princess?" I opened the drawer and pulled out two leather bound journals.

"When you put it that way...." Jared took one of the journals and plopped down on the bed, ignoring my protest over disturbing Pru's room. He opened the first volume of my sister's private thoughts, flipping pages like a speed reader. "None of these entries are about her. That's a bit strange, don't you think?"

I ignored his pointed question and flipped through the journal, stopping on random pages until I read enough to form my own conclusion. Unfortunately, it was the same as Jared's. "Neither are these."

Dreamwalker.

The word hung unspoken between us.

"Ellie—."

"Don't." I snatched the diary from his hands before he had a chance to say anything else.

Oh Goddess, four weeks with Mr. Know It All, black magic user. If our first night together is any indication, I'll be lucky to survive the month.

Still, so far he was keeping his side of the bargain and I'd pay any price for Pru's safe return – even my clean aura.

With the journals clutched to my chest, I swallowed my pride and admitted defeat. "So, she's a dreamwalker. Now what?"

"Now we find out where she walked off to. What's the date on the last entry in each journal?" Jared shrugged off his pack and started rooting through its contents. He set a sachet and a pack of matches beside him on the bed.

"This one ends in June of last year. And this one...." I switched journals and flipped to the end. "December."

"Unless she stopped writing, there's a more recent volume hidden here somewhere." Jared struck the match and lit the sachet in a whoof of gray smoke.

"What are you doing? You're going to burn the guest house down and guess who'll take the blame for that?" I rushed to the kitchenette and filled a glass of water.

"I'm saving us time with a simple hide and seek spell." Jared mumbled something else in that almost Latin language.

"In case you didn't notice, I can't afford rent, never mind construction costs for a cottage." My hand was poised over the burning herbs, ready to douse the small flames when someone called my name.

"*Brujo*." Jared's cold greeting caught me off guard.

"His name is Hector, not Brujo." Without thinking, I rushed to give him a hug, splashing water on his shirt. "Oh, sorry." I brushed the few droplets that hadn't soaked in away and apologized again.

"Rosaria heard you were coming." Hector eyed the contained fire with suspicion as he handed me a thermos and brown paper bag with small grease stains on the side, its contents still warm.

"Is this what I think it is?" I opened the bag and inhaled the sweet scent of fried deliciousness.

"You're going to bring her home. I can feel it." Hector's smile reached his eyes but his attention was on Jared. "My grandfather was the *brujo* in our village when I was a boy. I like to think it's in my blood but I never had the gift. Rosaria and I, we knew what Ellie was the moment she walked through that door." Hector pointed toward the main house. "Just like I know what you are."

Jared outstretched his arms. "I've never pretended to be anything more or less."

Hector rested hands calloused from long years laboring on the Harris property on my shoulders. "Ellie, there is darkness around him. I can feel it."

"He's helping me find Pru." I steeled my spine against the judgment in Hector's eyes.

"Got it." Jared leapt from the bed and dragged the ottoman from in front of the overstuffed arm chair to the side of the bed. He pushed up on one of the coffered ceiling tiles and reached inside the ceiling to retrieve another journal.

"Mrs. Harris wanted to know how long you planned on staying. Mr. Harris, he has a meeting with the chief of police for a progress report about Prudence. She said it would be better if you weren't here when the chief arrives." Hector's brows knitted together as a scowl formed on his face.

"Don't get upset on my account. I'm used to it." I shrugged off the Harris's dismissal. "I'm used to it. Wouldn't want the police to find out they've consulted a witch."

"You can tell Babs we're done here." Jared snuffed out the smoldering herbs with his hands, shoving the remnants of his magic use and the journals in his backpack.

"I hope you know what you're doing." Hector wrapped his arm around me and steered me toward the door. "I passed on what I could, you know?"

I wrapped my arm around Hector's middle in a half hug, squeezing as tight as I could. "You and Rosaria were the best part of growing up here."

Hector squeezed me back as he ushered me out the door. "We would have taken you—."

"It's okay." I would have gone with them. Rosaria and Hector were good people but their lives were tied to the Harris's. They lived and worked on the estate. "Everything is going to be okay."

I knew he would smell the lie but I needed to hear it as much as he did.

Hector escorted us across the lawn and up the cement steps to the back of the house where Jared's bike waited for us. Rosaria rushed out of the servant's entrance and wrapped me in a hug tight enough to bruise my ribs.

"I prayed the rosary every day for Mrs. Harris to ask for your help searching for Prudence. Hector gave you the thermos? And the empanadas?" She released me from the bear hug and held me at arm's length for a thorough once over. "You're too thin, *mija*. And you...." Finished with her appraisal of my condition, she turned her attention to my companion. Jared paled under the intensity of her gaze. "Hector may not be a *brujo* but that doesn't mean I don't know any. If something happens to her—."

"Rosaria." I stepped in front of her to block her view of Jared and stop her before she made the mistake of threatening a black magic user because of me. "I'm going to do everything I can to find Pru and bring her home. Nothing's going to happen to me. I promise."

One day I'd learn not to make promises I couldn't keep.

Chapter Seven

The two-wheeled death machine rumbled to life. Jared kept it balanced while I climbed on what marginally passed for a passenger seat. I'd never missed my beat up, backfiring truck more than when I straddled that race bike. Helmet secured, I wrapped my arms around his waist and held on for dear life as he peeled out of the staff parking lot and down the long drive. Without waiting for the iron gate to fully extend, he maneuvered the bike through the narrow opening and left the Heights behind.

I would do anything to find Pru but I hoped that was my last visit to the Harris estate. One trip down memory lane was enough.

Jared turned off the com units inside the helmets, sparing himself from my squeals of terror and prayers to the Goddess as he leaned the bike into the turns at death defying speeds. Still, it would have been nice to ask where we were going before he dropped me off in front of one of the shadiest hotels in Gaston.

I flipped the helmet visor up so he could see the indignation in my eyes. "Maybe the fact I'm currently living out of my truck gave you the wrong impression, Adams, but I am not the kind of girl who just goes off to a seedy motel with a guy she barely knows."

"Maybe the seedy motel gave *you* the wrong impression." Jared reached into his back pocket for his wallet and pulled out a few twenties. "We need to lay low—they rent rooms by the hour and take cash."

"You mean, *you* need a place to lay low." I grabbed the cash and stormed off in the direction of the red neon flashing sign that would have read "OFFICE" if three letters weren't burnt out.

I avoided the engine oil slicked puddles as I crossed the empty parking lot and yanked on the glass door of the office. It didn't budge. An open sign hung from a dingy suction cup, mocking me from the other side. I tugged again. The night clerk, engrossed in whatever show he was watching on the tablet propped up on the counter, didn't so much as look in my direction while I struggled to get inside.

"Mind the door. It sticks." The sound of gun fire and car crashes paused as the clerk touched the tablet screen with his pointer finger.

"I need a roo—." The door swung closed and smacked me in the backside, knocking me two steps forward.

"I said mind the door." The clerk scratched the inside of his ear and examined his finger before wiping it across the front of his shirt. He spun the guest book around. "How long?"

"How much for a double occupancy?" I counted the twenties Jared gave me.

"We only got singles. King or queen?" The clerk's nicotine stained teeth poked through his mangy mustache when he smiled. "How long?"

"However long this will get me." I slapped the money on the counter and spun the guest registry around.

Based on the list of questionable names, we weren't the only ones hiding out at the Crescent Park Motel. After signing as Andrea Jackson, a cleverly devised pseudonym based on my method of payment, I spun the book back around and waited for the clerk to count the money and hand over a key.

"Check out's at noon." He slid the key to room sixteen across the grimy counter. "Up the stairs and around the back."

"Thanks." I took the key, unable to hide the shudder and look of disgust when he ran a finger across the top of my hand.

Key in hand, I barreled into the door, putting all my weight behind it to ensure it opened and made a hasty retreat. Jared waited for me at the end of the sidewalk closest to the stairs.

I tossed him the key. "Next time you check in."

His expression darkened as his hand closed around the key. "Why? What did Henry do?"

"You're on a first name basis with that guy?" I waved off my last statement. "Never mind. Of course you are."

The preview of my four week term with Jared left little to be desired.

"What the hell is that supposed to mean?" Jared sounded genuinely offended but his attention was still on the motel's office – and Henry.

"It means...." I opened my arms, gesturing to everything around us. "This is about what I expected. I have to say, I'm a little disappointed after the nice guy routine back in your workshop."

"Well, that makes two of us who are disappointed. You're not even half the witch I thought you were." Jared turned his focus from the office and saw the hurt I knew was written all over my face.

I slung the first insult and should have expected him to react. Still, his words stung. Probably because they were true. As far as witches went, my magic was a disappointment.

Jared jammed the key into the lock, opening the door with more force than necessary and stomping inside the dark and dingy motel room. I reached inside, fingers fumbling along the wall until they came into contact with the light switch and something sticky that I tried not to over analyze. The yellow fluorescent light revealed worn carpet, peeling wallpaper, and threadbare blankets on the single queen size bed.

"This is romantic. I can see now why it's such a popular place." I muttered to myself as I set my bag on the small table opposite the bed.

Jared's mouth turned up in a half smile but he didn't laugh or otherwise acknowledge my comment. He plopped down on the bed, kicked off his boots, pulled one of Pru's journals out of his bag, and settled in to read.

Rather than saddle up next to him, I made a quick stop in the bathroom which was marginally cleaner than expected before setting up camp at the table. I reached into my bag for the other dream diary we found in Pru's cottage. My stomach growled as my fingers brushed past Rosaria's care package. The empanadas. I'd almost forgotten.

I grabbed the thermos and grease stained bag from my pack, poured myself a cup of the warm café au lait, and ate one cold, apple stuffed fried pastry in two bites. The second and third empanada went down just as easily. The fourth, not so much. My stomach grumbled its discontent. Too much, too soon. I nursed the coffee and started reading.

I ignored my gastrointestinal distress, the awkward tension sucking the oxygen out of the room, and the pins and needles in my butt from sitting in the uncomfortable wooden chair, and read every entry my sister wrote. Jared did the same from what surely had to be a more comfortable position on the bed.

At least I was less likely to get hepatitis while sitting at the table.

My invasion of Pru's privacy began almost a year prior in the spring. Some of her journal entries were mundane, some were terrifying, but each passage was written with the same flourish as if she were addressing a penpal. But more curious than the formal way she wrote each entry was their subject matter.

Not a single one was about her.

While Pru was absent from her own dreams, there were two women who appeared over and over again. One of them was clearly in danger from the other. I couldn't make out who they were but *what* they were was obvious.

Witches.

Oh, Prudence. Why didn't you tell me what was going on? The entries became more disturbing with each passing night. One woman hunting the other. Each night she gained ground, closing in on her prey, until she had her in her clutches, devouring her magic in a carnivorous display.

Tears tracked down my cheeks as I set the diary on the table. Pru managed to put on a happy face while plagued with such violent and terrifying nightmares. She was the better, the stronger, of the two of us and it had cost her everything.

Unable to stomach the sweet smell of the apple empanadas or the rich café au lait after everything I read, I pushed the treats to the other side of the table.

"You're not going to finish those?" Jared set his copy of Pru's journal on the bed beside him and eyed the food on the table.

Neither of us had spoken since our little spat in the parking lot. It seemed Jared was an equal match when it came to being stubborn. Still, he wasn't the source of my anger or frustration. That laid squarely with my lack of progress. I was no closer to finding Pru than when I started. Which wasn't an excuse for starving the person trying to help – even if it did cost me four weeks of freedom.

"Help yourself." I tossed the grease stained paper bag at Jared. "Find anything useful?"

The hope of discovering a viable lead in one of Pru's journals soured along with the food in my stomach. The book he read was no doubt more of the same. Or was it?

Jared hesitated, his gaze shifting from me to the journal and back again. He dropped the bag as if the contents burned him and snatched the book of the bed, clutching it to his chest. Jared went from ally to suspect in a flash. What was he hiding?

All the anger, fear and frustration bubbled to the surface – along with something else. Something wild and untamable. My magic. It roiled inside me, begging to be unleashed with a veracity I hadn't felt since the Harris's discovered what I was. Overcome with emotion and energy, I gave it what it wanted.

A target.

The magic surged through my body only to fizzle out on contact with Jared. It was a small shock, rather than the high voltage I aimed for. Still, it was enough to force him to drop Pru's journal. It hit the floor and landed on its spine. The book began to split at the center, its pages fluttering in dramatic fashion until it laid open at the center and revealed its secrets. One word was scrawled over and over again across the two pages.

My name.

"Is it all like this?" Without waiting for an answer, I dropped to my knees and picked up the book, flipping through its pages. The second half of her journal was nothing but my name, her handwriting deteriorating with each page I turned. "You saw this back at Pru's and didn't say anything. Why?"

"I didn't want to scare you." Jared held out a hand to help me to my feet. "I thought I'd find something... more. I have no idea what that means."

He looked me dead in the eye and lied.

I swatted his hand away and gripped the journal tighter. "You're lying."

"I'm lying? Really? I'm trying to help you." Jared did a better than average job of pretending to be offended.

I wasn't buying the act.

It was a good thing, too, because Jared was a snake oil salesman and the snake was standing right outside our motel room door.

"Knock, knock, knock." The singsong voice spoke in time with the raps on the hollow door. "Room service."

"Shit, it's Helene." Jared grabbed my arm, yanked me up from the floor, and shoved me inside the tiny closet in our room. "Stay here."

"She's a witch, Jared. She'll find me. And why am I the one hiding? She's after you." I asked, confused why our roles weren't reversed.

He pulled a small knife from his pocket and sliced his left palm. Ignoring me and my numerous questions about why I was in the closet, he dipped his fingers in the blood pooling in his cupped hand and wrote symbols on the inside of the closet door. He wrote a symbol on my forehead and ran a bloodied thumb across my lips. I tried to protest, to scream my objection to being shoved in a closet and blood smeared across my face but nothing happened. I couldn't move or talk.

Again.

You son of a bitch. You better hope I never get a lock of your hair....

Jared seemed to pick up on my thoughts. The look of daggers I shot at him may have played a role. "I'll explain everything. I promise. Please, Ellie." Jared pleaded, before shoving the braided lock of my hair in the front pocket of my jeans.

If my arms worked, I would have throat punched him.

Interesting things happen when you're immobilized and alone inside a tiny closet in a seedy motel room. It's dark, you can't see anything, but you find clarity. It's quiet, you don't make a sound, but you hear everything. And what I heard ignited every cell in my body.

Jared set me up. The question was why. If I wanted to survive and save my sister, I needed to find the answer. There was just one problem – I was trapped in a closet.

Chapter Eight

Three more rapid knocks preceded Helene's entrance into the motel room. "Jared, just hand over the girl. Things will go much smoother if you just do what I hired you to do. Don't make me come in there and get her myself."

The knowledge that Jared worked for Helene cut deep. Almost as deep as the realization I'd never find Prudence once he handed me over to her.

"Oh, come on, Helene, it wouldn't be the first time you got your hands dirty." Jared replied. The chain jangled against the door as he fumbled with the locks.

"But I just had a manicure." Helene complained. "It's a lovely shade of red – the blood of my enemies. Now, where's the girl?"

Jared cleared his throat. "I lost her."

"You lost her?" Helene asked, disbelief heavy in her voice.

"I dozed off reading her sister's journal. She must have dipped out while I was asleep."

"He fell asleep. Do you believe that?" Helene spoke to someone other than Jared, I assumed one of the two goons she had with her back at the store.

"I set a ward on the door but forgot about the window. It was open when I got up."

The worn shag carpet was enough to muffle the footsteps but I managed to make out three sets. Two clomped passed the closet door, confirming my suspicions about Helene's backup. The third was softer with the distinct sound of a high heel snagging in the carpet fibers. The window slammed shut.

They turned and walked back in the direction of the door but this time they stopped at the closet. My heart raced, pounding so hard, so loud, it threatened to give me away before they even opened the door.

The knob turned. The sound of my own blood pumping was deafening. Light rushed in, chasing away the dark shroud I hid behind.

Helene found what she was looking for.

One of her goons stepped forward, blocking some of the light and my view of the room with his blocky frame. "Empty." He slammed the door hard enough to rattle its hinges.

"You have twelve hours left on your contract, Jared. You read and agreed to the terms." Helene snapped her fingers and the sounds of someone choking followed. "I suggest you find her and bring her to me."

There was a loud thump as something heavy hit the floor.

"I want this wrapped up before the end of the lunar cycle. Don't disappoint me, Jared. Things get messy when I'm disappointed." Helene snapped her fingers again and called for her bodyguards. "Come along, boys, I want to stop at the apothecary for a fresh bundle of belladonna."

Belladonna? Helene has Pru? Of course she does.

Anger and betrayal fueled a fire within me until it raged wild and threatened to burst from my body; annihilating everything and everyone around me. Magic built behind the emotions, dousing the flames with gasoline rather than water. The pressure built and built, pushing against muscle, sinew, and bone. It reached the surface, searing my skin from the inside out and consuming all the oxygen in my lungs. Multicolored dots danced along the corners of my vision.

Of all the ways I thought I'd go, spontaneous human combustion never made the list. Witch dies in closet in ironic twist. Burned to death by her own magic.

When the pressure became too much, I blinked out of consciousness. Within seconds, having consumed all the oxygen and energy within me, the fire snuffed itself out. But the damage was done. With nowhere to run and no way to defend myself, my emotions and magic left me hollow – a charred and desolate wasteland on the inside.

My muscles burned for an entirely different reason. Not from the flames of my feelings but exhaustion. I would have collapsed, curled up into the fetal position inside the cramped closet and wept if not for Jared's spell. *Curse was more like it.*

Right on cue, the betrayer opened the closet door. "Ellie, I...." He looked at me, a spark of fear in his eyes, and took one step back, no doubt rethinking his decision to reverse his spell. "I know you're upset."

Under statement of the century. The blood he smeared across my lips cracked and began to flake away. His magic was unraveling. Had I done that? I didn't know and I didn't care. The second I was freed from his spell I was out of there. I didn't have a lot of magic but I had a hell of a right cross.

"Ellie, you have to believe me, I didn't have a choice. I was a dead man if I refused her contract and I'm a dead man if I don't deliver. You're the best shot I have of walking away from this."

The spell dissolved and I rocked into motion. My fist hit his jaw with less oomph than normal due to my exhaustion and the cramped space but it was enough to hurtle him backwards. He hit the wall and slid the rest of the way down to the carpet.

"Only one of us is walking away, Jared." I stumbled out of the closet on wobbly legs and stepped over him, resting a hand on the corner of the mattress for stability as I made my way to the table. By the grace of the Goddess I managed to grab my things and walk out of the motel room. The street lights and motel's flashing neon sign assaulted my eyes after being trapped in the dark but I trudged through the puddles, avoiding potholes as I crossed the parking lot.

I made it to the street corner before Jared caught up with me.

"She owns me, Ellie." He stepped in front of me. "The store, the building, everything. I sold her a fake relic and she bought out my entire life."

"So, you thought, what? You'd trade your life for mine?" I bumped him with my shoulder as I brushed past. "You're a real gentleman, Adams. A regular fucking hero."

"I had plenty of opportunities to hand you over. She'd already have you if that's what I wanted." Jared called after me but didn't give chase. "You can't run. You can't hide. Not on your own. She'll find you."

"Good." I hitched my backpack up on my shoulder and kept walking.

Jared flashed in front of me, blocking my route of escape. "Good?"

"At least then I'll have a shot at saving Pru. Now move." I tried to push him out of the way with little success.

Jared let out a sarcastic laugh. "You have no idea who she is or what she's capable of. You've got no clue what you're talking about."

"You're right. I don't. That might have something to do with the fact you've been lying and working against me this whole time." I shoved him again, putting what little magic I had behind it.

Which turned out, for once, to be quite a lot.

Jared flew backward, tumbling into the dumpster on the other side of the parking lot. The result was unexpected but rather than question the power surge, I seized the opportunity and got the hell out of there. Cauldron Crafts was only a few blocks away. Which meant I was only a few blocks away from my truck.

I'm not big on running – unless it was from my problems. My lungs and muscles burned but I kept pushing. I ran like my life depended on it because for once it actually did. Cutting through Crescent Park shortened the trip by a quarter mile. The old carousel came in to view as I rounded the last corner. A large swath of grass, half a dozen picnic tables, and several city trash cans were all that separated me from my truck. I slowed to a jog, hoping to avoid any unwanted attention from the park's nighttime inhabitants. For the most part my neighbors left me alone and I was all too happy to return the favor.

But that didn't mean they wouldn't rat you out for a hot meal or a quick fix.

The park benches were deserted. Not entirely unusual given the average nighttime temperature but my senses were on high alert. Something felt off. I reached around and unzipped the small pocket on my backpack and fished out my keys, clenching my fist around all but one key. With the ignition key between my index and middle finger, I had a makeshift dagger and a small amount of confidence. I widened my stride, cutting across the park on a diagonal, and hopped the small boxwood hedge lining the sidewalk to shave precious seconds off my time.

No one jumped out of the shadows but I couldn't shake the feeling someone was watching, waiting for the right time to grab me and hand me over to Helene. Landing in her clutches now would end any chance I had of saving Pru. The next time I saw the witch I wanted it to be on my terms, when I was ready.

But I was far from ready and the clock was ticking.

A single lane of asphalt was all that separated me from my truck. "Your rust and bald tires never looked so good." I ran a hand along the faded paint. "You're going to start on the first try and we're going to drive out of here, okay?" The pep talk was as much for me as it was my truck.

"You missed our appointment." A man's voice came from behind a tree by the parking pace two spots over.

"Shit." Startled, I dropped the keys while trying to unlock the truck door. I'd never coveted a key fob more than in that moment.

"You never miss an appointment." Shadows from the tree's canopy blocked his face as he stepped out onto the sidewalk but I recognized his voice.

"Sam? What are you doing here?" I bent down to grab my keys.

That was a classic b-horror movie mistake.

Sam closed the distance between us and backed me up against the driver's side door. "You missed our appointment. I waited."

"Our appointment isn't until Friday. It's only Tues...." I looked up at the brightening sky. "It's Wednesday. How long have you been here? Is something wrong?"

Of course, something's wrong. There is nothing right about a man you barely know waiting in the dark for you to show up. I noticed Sam's eyes, glazed over with a white film typical of someone being ridden by dark magic about the same time I decided it was time for my least favorite exercise – running.

But it was too late for that.

Sam grabbed me by the neck and squeezed. The pressure built from my esophagus to the back of my eyes. I sucked in what little air I could and prayed to the Goddess I had enough energy to zap his ass like I had Jared.

It would have been a great plan if my magic wasn't hit or miss.

I came up empty in the magical department but I wasn't empty-handed. Jabbing a client in the neck with your car keys isn't good for business but desperate times called for desperate measures. I stabbed him once behind the collar bone and once in the neck before he loosened his grip. After the third puncture in the shoulder he let me go. The white haze over his eyes melted away, along with the black magic that had been cast on him.

I slid down the truck, still gasping for air, until I my ass hit the pavement and broke my fall. Fueled by adrenaline, I dropped to my stomach, rolled under the truck, and popped out the other side.

"Where am I?" Sam's brow was furrowed, his fingers coming away covered in blood as he touched the spot on his neck where I stabbed him. "What's going on? Ellie? Is that you?"

I nodded, raising my arms slowly as if held at gun point and stepping under the streetlight. "It's okay, Sam."

"What are you doing? Were you trying to rob me?" He started to pat himself down, checking for his personal items when he noticed the red marks on my neck. His gaze shifted from me to his hands and back again. "I did that to you."

"It's okay." I lied. Again. None of it was okay. "I won't press charges. Just… just go home, Sam. I'm not going to call the cops. Just go home."

Taking care not to startle him, I kept my movements slow, unlocking the passenger side door and climbing inside. After locking the door behind me, I slid across the bench seat, started the truck and shifted into reverse. Still in a fog from the spell, Sam didn't move. I tried one last time to get him to move.

"Sam, I will back this truck right over your feet. Go home." I didn't know what or who Sam had waiting at home for him or what would happen when he got there for that matter but I didn't care. We all had our problems.

Mine started with a capital h – Helene.

Most witches would have cast a spell and wiped his memory of the whole thing. I wasn't most witches. I was barely a witch by most witches' standards. So, instead of bewitching him, Sam and I had a hellish two minutes neither of us would forget.

"I… I'm sorry." For once, he actually heeded my advice and hauled ass.

So did I.

With no destination in mind, I made a right on Arbor Street and drove until the engine sputtered, the arrow pointing at the E of the gas gauge mocking me. After shifting into neutral, I drifted into a truck stop parking lot off Highway 9 and pushed my old rust bucket the rest of the way to the fuel pump.

Out of gas and out of time, I needed a plan – and fast. Pru didn't have long and if Helene's actions were any indication, neither did I.

After grabbing a spare tarot deck from the glove compartment, I sat on the tailgate and shuffled the cards while my truck guzzled down gasoline. I never read my cards. Ever. It was an unwritten reader's rule. Knowing your future clouded your judgment and the ability to see the future of others.

But rules were meant to be broken.

A traditional Celtic Cross was the go-to for my regular readings but I wasn't looking to shed light on all of my problems. I had way too many issues for that. Specific situations call for specific spreads and in my case I needed the Star Guide.

Eight cards.

Not one of them had the answer I needed. I reshuffled the deck and tried again with the same results. So, I tried again and again, hoping for a different reading, but nothing changed. Present situation – sucked. Cause of conflict or obstacle – obvious. Helene. Changes needed in order to overcome obstacles – me. Strength – magic. *Doubtful.* Other challenges – Jared.

Final outcome – completely screwed.

The gas pump beeped, alerting me that the tank was full just in time to prevent gas from overflowing. I scooped up my cards, wrapped them back up in the swath of crushed velvet, and shoved them in my jacket pocket for safekeeping until I got back in the truck.

"Isn't there a rule about reading your own cards?" Jared stepped out from behind the adjoining gas pump. "Not that I've ever cared about playing by the rules."

How did he find me so fast? Not that it mattered. If Jared was there, Helene wasn't far behind. Jared was right – and so were the cards. I couldn't beat her. Not at her own game. I had one card left to play if I wanted to get my sister back.

"Drop the flirty, bad boy act, Jared. We both know why you're here." Resigned to my fate, I steeled my spine and made an offer. "I have something your boss wants and I'm willing to trade it for Prudence."

"There's only one thing Helen wants." Jared shook his head. "Don't play dumb, Ellie. It doesn't suit you. You want to get Prudence back? Handing yourself over isn't going to accomplish that."

"She turned Sam into some sort of zombie looking thing and sent him after me. He tried to strangle me in front of your store. So, yeah, trading myself for Pru seems like the best option." I pulled the lock of hair out of my pocket. "You should have held on to this. You can't make me do anything. Not anymore. You've been working for her this whole time. Why should I listen to you?"

"I don't want you to do anything accept listen." Jared rubbed his jaw. "You throw a hell of a punch by the way. Wait—who the hell is Sam?"

"A regular. He gets a reading every week. She sent him to kill me." I pointed to the bruises on my neck.

"But he didn't." One corner of Jared's mouth turned up in a wry grin. "Oh, I bet Helene is pissed. That little spell cost her."

"Little spell? Maybe I hit you harder than I thought." I shook my head. "I had to stab him with my keys, Jared. More than once. I can't fight murderous mind control spells with a right hook. I can't trust you. Which shouldn't have come as a surprise but it did. So, there you go. Would you just make the call so I can make the trade?"

"She'll kill you and keep Prudence." Jared's tone brooked no argument.

Not that I've ever let that stop me.

"You don't know that." I walked around to the driver's side of the truck. "If you won't call her, I'll just head back to Crescent Park. One of Helene's goons is bound to show up looking for me. Maybe they'll take me to her."

"Maybe they'll finish what your *friend* Sam started." Jared opened the passenger side door and climbed in without waiting for an invitation.

Which made sense because I had no intention of offering one.

"He's a client. Not a *friend*." I snapped, mocking the emphasis Jared put on the word. "Now get out of my truck."

"Defiant right to the end. And it will be your end, Ellie." Jared got out and slammed the door. "By the way, Helene is your cousin. Twice removed or something. Your family tree has a lot of branches. Oh, and she killed your mother."

"Playing on the foster kid's desperation for information about her family? That's low, Jared, even for you. For the record, I outgrew that dream years ago." I got in the truck and started the engine, keeping one eye on Jared in the side mirror as I drove off in the direction of Highway 9.

He's lying. He has to be lying. But oh, Goddess, what if he isn't?

I cut the wheel, bald tires squealing against the pavement in protest as I turned around in the middle of the road and headed back to the truck stop for Jared. I pulled up to the same pump where I'd left him and rolled the window down. "Get in."

"Glad you came to your senses." Jared settled into the passenger seat, pulling the seatbelt across his chest and fastening it into place like it would permanently secure his position by my side.

"Worried we'll get down the road and I'll try to toss you out of a moving vehicle?" I asked, only half joking.

"The thought crossed my mind." He leaned forward and fiddled with the heat.

"Jared, I swear to the Goddess, stop messing with my truck and tell me what you know about Helene or I will show you exactly what I did to Sam – and I actually liked him."

"Calm down—."

"In your experience, when has telling a woman to calm down actually helped the situation?" I asked, jerking the wheel to the right as I tore out of the parking lot and headed back toward the highway.

"Probably never." Jared laughed as he turned in the seat to face me. "Like I was saying, you and Helene are related. You're both named after the same ancestor. Well, some variation of Ellen's name anyway. A true family of witches. That's pretty rare. I don't know if you've noticed but over the last three centuries we've become a solitary bunch."

"Witch hunts will do that to you." I muttered. "I thought you said people brought their kids to you for lessons?"

One corner of his mouth upturned in a lopsided grin at my offhand comment. "They do but that's not the same as a coven. Now, I'm not indoctrinated in coven culture, having never been in one myself, but from what I've read, magic is evenly distributed between members. It's all about the balance, the order of things." He paused a beat, waiting to see if I was following along. Accepting my nod as confirmation, he continued with his story. "Communal witches. It sounds great, right?" Jared shook his head as if the exact opposite were true. "I'm sure it was for a while but that's too much power in one place. Inquisitions weren't the only thing destroying covens. Witches were doing it to themselves."

"Not that this isn't a fascinating history lesson but what does this have to do with me and Helene?" I flicked the turn signal on and merged into traffic with no destination in mind.

"I'm getting to that. Where are we going?" Jared asked as he reached down and pulled an old leather-bound book out of his backpack.

"Nowhere in particular. I just thought it would be better not to stay in one place until we had a plan." I spared a glance in his direction before focusing on the road again.

"Good idea." He set the book between us on the bench seat, resting a hand on its cover. "A few years ago, I came across an old grimoire. It was filled with spells – old ones. Even the margins had scribblings in them. Most of them were variations of spell and curses I was already familiar with but there was one I'd never seen before."

"And?" I prompted when he seemed to drift off in his own thoughts.

"It's black magic, Ellie." Jared's shudder sent chills up my spine. He practiced black magic and the spell gave him pause. That wasn't a good sign. "It wasn't crafted with ill intent but in the wrong hands, in Helene's hands, it is the most dangerous spell I've ever seen."

I was almost too afraid to ask. "What does it do?"

"Takes the power from one witch and gives it to another." He picked up the tome and opened the front cover. "That's not the worst part."

"How is that not the worst part? I didn't know someone could do that. Why would you do that?" The stream of consciousness poured from my mouth as I tried to process what he said.

"It's part of a funeral rite. When a witch died the coven would perform the ritual and the magic would be redistributed within the community."

"Like a magical recycling program?" I asked.

"Yeah, exactly. Except Helene didn't want to wait for Mother Nature to take her course." Jared rested a hand on the open grimoire.

"Holy Hecate. She's killing witches and consuming their power." I checked the side mirrors to be sure we weren't followed as a wave of paranoia washed over me.

"But that's not the worst—."

"Goddess, Jared. How much worse does it get? Quit dragging it out and get to the damned point." Nerves and a healthy dose of fear made my palms sweat and driving difficult.

"You're the last witch she needs to kill." Jared braced against the dash as I slammed on the brakes. "We're in the middle of the highway, Ellie."

My breaths came in quick shallow bursts as I bordered on hyperventilating. "Prudence?"

"I think Prudence was dreamwalking, stumbled onto something about you, and chased it. Helene found her first." Jared cleared his throat. "Ellie, we're still in the middle of the road."

A tractor trailer blew by on the right with his air horn blaring. I moved my foot from the brake to the gas and veered us off to the shoulder.

"And my... mother?" I choked on the word, terrified he would confirm what I knew in my heart – Helene killed her.

"It's just a theory but I think she gave you up before Helene..." Jared noticed the color draining from my face, grabbed a half empty bottle of water that rolled out from under the seat and made me drink it. "The stuff we were working on back at my shop, it was more than just teaching you rudimentary magic. I needed to see if I was right."

"Right about what?" I wiped the back of my hand across my mouth, catching an errant drop of water.

"You're in a bind." Jared took the empty bottle of water and shoved it in the door pocket.

"Um, I'm not the only one." I waved a finger between us and chuckled. "If I'm in a bind so are you."

"Not in a bind, like bad situation, although technically that does apply here, *in a bind*." Jared emphasized the words, slowing his speech down as if that would help me decode. At my blank expression he sighed. "Your magic is blocked. Someone, I can only assume it was your mother, cast a spell to put a knot in your aura choking off your power. Except in your case it was more of a kink than a knot since you've been leaking magic."

"Leaking magic? That's why any attempt at a spell ends in catastrophe and my best skill is tarot?" My head spun. It was too much.

"It's a working theory. I don't have any real proof except the bind. I can feel it, like you have a second pulse. If I can sense it, Helene will, too, and she'll capitalize on it." Jared tapped the book again. "But we can fix that. There's a spell here—."

"I feel sick." I scrambled out of the truck as my stomach rejected the water I'd guzzled down.

Jared was at my side in a flash, holding my hair back with one hand and rubbing the small of my back with the other as I retched on the side of the road. The fact that it was the most romantic moment of my life spoke volumes.

"It's a lot to absorb. I'm sorry, really. I didn't plan to hit you with this all at once." Jared waited for the heaves to subside before he dropped the next bomb on me. "You should have come into your full seat of power on your sixteenth birthday. Right around the time all your problems started at home."

"So that's why you wanted a month. You were hoping to figure out what was wrong with my magic before Helene got her hands on me." I used the hem of my jacket and wiped my mouth. "Can you see if there's any gum in the glove box?"

"Gum?" Jared asked, puzzled.

"You're a double agent. There's a witch trying to kill me and suck the magic from my corpse. The same witch who has Prudence and killed my mother. It's a lot to take in, Jared. I'd rather not do it with vomit breath."

A girl has to have her priorities in a crisis situation.

"Fair enough." With one last pat on the back he climbed into the truck and rummaged around while I braced myself on the side of the road and contemplated the state of my life. "No gum. Just a peppermint candy out of its wrapper."

I took the mint, picked off the unknown fuzz stuck to its side, and popped it in my mouth. "I need to reevaluate my plan."

"You mean the one where you hand yourself over to Helene? The one that ended in certain death?" Jared leaned against the side of the truck with his arms crossed over his chest.

"Yes, *that one*." Stomach empty and legs stable, I deemed it safe to leave the road side and walked over to the truck.

Jared stepped in front of me. "How about letting me drive for a while?"

Something about the way he asked led me to believe he had a destination in mind. "Let me guess, you have a plan."

"Sort of." Jared winked and hauled himself up into the driver's seat.

Goddess help me, I let Jared take the wheel and climbed into the passenger side. A broken witch, a practitioner of dark arts, and the grimoire that started it all.

What could possibly go wrong?

Chapter Ten

"This is it." Jared pulled up alongside a dilapidated two-story stone home on the outskirts of Gaston City.

"This is what?" I asked, climbing out of the truck to stretch my legs after the forty-minute drive. "Condemned?"

The sun crested the horizon, highlighting the missing slate shingles and shutters hanging half off their hinges. Shrubs and vines overtook the front steps which were missing two boards. The gutters were supported only by the downspouts on either end, sagging away from the roof.

"The ancestral home." With the grimoire tucked under his arm, Jared made his way to the porch.

"Oh, well, I love what your family's done with the place. It's... quaint. Very Addams Family." My foot caught in the vines while trying to avoid falling through the broken steps. I landed on the porch with a thud after losing my fight with the foliage.

Jared looked down to see me sprawled out on the rotten porch boards and smiled before offering a hand up. "Not my family, Ellie."

"Mine." I brushed some of the dirt and grime from my jeans. "Of course it is."

Years of neglect and weather damage rendered the lock on the front door useless. The wood splintered in two, leaving the doorknob in Jared's hand while the rest swung open.

"Ladies first." He made a sweeping gesture, motioning for me to lead the way.

"And they say chivalry is dead." I crossed the threshold, swiping at spiderwebs as I made my way inside.

While rot and vines overtook the outside of the house, the interior remained intact. A thin layer of dust and cobwebs coated everything but the floorboards were solid and none of the stairs were missing. The first floor spilt off in three directions from the foyer. Straight ahead was a long hallway with two doors on the right side. Sliding doors revealed parlors on either side.

I veered left, drawn to a faded portrait of a woman with similar features to mine hung above the fireplace. The clothes and hairstyle dated her well beyond an age to be my mother but there was no denying our relation. The shape of her eyes, curve of her lips, and slight upturn at the tip of her nose were more than enough proof.

"You look like her." Jared stopped to admire the painting as well.

"With the right corset and several hundred bobbypins we could pass for twins." I reached for a small silver frame on the mantle and wiped the dust coating the glass.

Dressed for a sunny summer day in the late sixties, early seventies, the woman in that photo looked back at me with the same features. She was about the right age. I couldn't help but wonder if the woman with the bright eyes and unsuspecting smile fell prey to Helene. Was she my mother?

"The James women have strong genes." Jared placed a hand at the small of my back and nudged me toward the next room. "We don't have a lot of time. Helene will know we're here as soon as I start the spell."

"If this works... I mean, if we make it out of this alive, I'd like to...." I didn't bother to finish the sentence. It was too much to hope for a happy ending.

"No one is going to stop you from coming back here. All we have to do is survive the next six hours. And kill Helene." Jared shrugged the subject of murder off like it was regular conversation around the dinner table.

"Simple as that, huh? Just kill the witch. No big deal." I prayed I never became so indifferent to taking someone's life.

Even if they did deserve it.

He held open the swinging door separating the parlor from the kitchen. "She broke the creed and defied the Goddess. Her magic is toxic and there's no coming back from that. If I thought there was another way... but there isn't. I've looked."

"Why here?" I lingered in the parlor, sparing one last look at the portrait above the fireplace.

"It's a seat of power. You have a connection to this place." Jared chose to rephrase his words at my skeptical expression. "This house is connected to you. It doesn't matter that you don't remember it."

"Okay, we'll go with that. As for the rest, I'm a little sketchy on the details. You undo the spell blocking my magic. Helene shows up and what? We have some sort of magical showdown? How is this better than my plan?" I brushed past him into the kitchen.

"Unlike yours, my plan has a moderate chance for success." Jared set the grimoire on a roughhewn wooden table in the center of the room. "I'd kill for a workspace like this."

"Well, here's your chance. Courtesy of Helene." I feigned indifference but truth be told the kitchen was a witch's dream.

An old cast iron cauldron hung from a rounded hearth. Glass jars filled the shelves in an open storeroom on the far-right side. Bowls and pots of varying sizes lined a shelf above the gas range and there was an island with a butcher block top in the center of the room. Herbs and flowers hung from the wood beams across the entire ceiling. Petals, crushed leaves, and other pieces of plant matter littered the floor like natural confetti from the critters that had taken up residence after the house had been abandoned.

"Sorry, poor choice of words." Jared brushed the plant debris from the work table before setting the grimoire and his backpack down. "Let's get started. Grab one of those bowls over there."

"Don't we need like a cleansing ritual or something?" I asked as I stood on tiptoe, stretching to reach a clay bowl on the shelf. I freed two from their dusty prison but only one survived. I winced as the second bowl hit the floor and sent shards of pottery everywhere.

"Normally, yes, but we're on a deadline. So we're just going to have to get down and dirty." Jared set a small sampling of his personal stock stored in plastic vials on the work surface.

"There's more than one joke in there." Pieces of broken bowl crunched under foot as I walked the few steps to the center island. "What's the first step?"

He flipped to the required spell, tracing the lines of text with his index finger as he reviewed each step. "It says the witch must be laid bare. You need to take off your clothes."

"What? Why? I can't see how me being naked is going to make a difference." I reached for the book, spinning it around so I could read the spell for myself. "It doesn't say anything about taking my clothes off."

Jared wore a devilish grin as he winked at me. "It was worth a shot." He turned the book around to face him. "It just means you have to remove any charms or amulets. Take off anything that can interfere with the spell."

"I sewed a couple gris-gris into the liner for protection." I slipped out of my jacket and tossed it on the counter behind me. "Worked like a charm." *Not.*

"If puns and bad taste could stop Helene, we'd be all set." Jared found a mortar and pestle in usable condition, placed the different ingredients inside, and crushed them all together until a gummy paste was formed. After scraping two fingers around the inside of the marble mortar, he wadded the paste into a little cube. "I was going to brew this, sort of like a broth or a tea. Maybe you should just eat it."

"Well, it looks delicious. The way you smushed it all up with your dirty hands. Yum. I cannot wait to try it." I couldn't keep a straight face, laughing as I plucked the magical gummy snack from his fingers and popped it in my mouth.

The combination of curry and pesto – two of my least favorite flavor profiles – kicked my gag reflex into high gear but I managed to choke it down. Out of reflex, I rushed to the faucet and turned on the water for a chaser. The pipes rattled and shook as the air in the lines forced a thick, muddy glop of water into the basin.

The well was dry.

"I guess it's a good thing the spell didn't require a liquid base. Do you feel anything yet?" Jared flipped to the next page in the grimoire.

"Besides sick?" I asked, swallowing back the saliva building in my mouth.

"Okay, so according to this, we just need to put you in a circle, candles at each direction... I'll read the words.... Got it." Jared fished a piece of chalk and four white tea lights from his bag.

"Aren't those for scented wax burners?" I picked up one of the candles, straightening the wick.

"Tapered are preferred for ceremonial purposes but they don't travel well. They break and then they're not worth a shit. There's a note scribble in the margin but I can't make it out. Something about blood?" He pointed to the handwriting in the margin.

I took the book and went to the window where there was better light. "Does that say circle?"

"A circle of blood." Jared peered over my shoulder. "Your blood."

"This just gets better and better. I have a thumb-knife on my keyring." I handed the book over to Jared and went for my keys.

"There's an athame in my bag." Jared kept a complete witch kit in his backpack. Of course he did.

Athame in my right hand, I sliced the blade across the palm of my left, pumped a fist to increase the blood flow, and walked a circle large enough for me to lay inside. Which was handy since I wanted to pass out afterward.

Jared took off his shirt and ripped one sleeve free. "I don't have any gauze but this will help stem the bleeding."

"Lying in a pool of my own blood wasn't how I envisioned this going." I positioned myself inside the circle like Davinci's Vitruvian Man.

"Now you're just being dramatic. It's not a pool of blood. It's barely half a pint." He struck a match against the floor and lit the candles. "So, how did you envision it?"

"I don't know, a wand? A little more bibidity-bobidity? A shower of sparkles." I closed my eyes and tried to imagine a fairy godmother but the only person I saw was Pru.

"You wanted the fairytale version?" Jared sounded surprised, as if a girl like me wouldn't believe in such silly things.

"It would be a nice change of pace."

"Yes," he admitted. "It would."

I guess we all wanted our happily ever after – even a black arts dealer.

"Ready?" Jared asked, grimoire in hand.

"As I'll ever be."

That was all the confirmation he needed. He read the spell, increasing in speed and volume as he said the words over and over. Pressure mounted in the room with each repetition. The leaves and debris scattered over the floor hovered in the air. Bowls and pots rattled on the shelves. The entire house shook.

And that was just outside the circle.

Within it everything amplified. Searing pain arced through my bones. Pressure built behind my eyes and inside my ears until I feared something would rupture. Spine bowed, I levitated several feet off the floor as my limbs were pulled in the direction of the four different candles.

The energy pulled back like a rubber band stretched to the limits of its elasticity, shattering the windows as it expanded beyond the kitchen. When it couldn't expand any further it snapped. The flow of energy reversed, crashing in on itself.

On me.

The world around me fell away in a flash of white light. All that remained was agony. All six senses were overrun. It became color, taste, smell, encompassing everything within view of the third eye. Time isn't reliable, it's relative. An hour of pleasure can feel like a minute. A minute of pain can feel like an eternity. I don't know how much time passed. I only know the number of times I prayed to the Goddess it would end. She never answered. Whatever happened to me, whatever pain I experienced, was part of her plan.

It would have been nice if she'd let me in on it.

"Ellie, can you hear me?" Jared straddled my waist as he pushed three times in the center of my chest. He titled my head back and pinched my nose closed. When his lips found mine, I took advantage of the situation.

Desperate times and dry spells call for desperate measures.

A girl doesn't come back from the brink of death only to possibly die again in a few hours without seizing the opportunity to kiss the hot guy – even if the hot guy is Jared.

I wrapped my arms around his neck, pulling him closer and deepening the kiss until I wasn't the only in need of help breathing.

He broke the kiss and the intoxication of a near death experience. "I thought you were dead. Your heart stopped." Desire was heavy in his eyes. He leaned in, lips brushing against mine before pulling back.

Almost dying can be an aphrodisiac. It can also be a wake-up call.

"I'm not dead yet." I pushed myself out from underneath him and sat up, half in, half out of the circle. "I'm not going to do Helene's work for her. If she wants me dead, she'll have to kill me herself."

"Someone came back from the grave full of piss and vinegar." Jared gave me a little wink. "Good."

"Well, you know what they say." I kept it cool, grateful we made an unspoken agreement not to discuss the kiss. "What doesn't kill you—."

"Gives you a jaded sense of humor and high probability for a drinking problem." Jared laughed but it held a bitter edge as if he spoke from experience.

"Not what I was going to say but highly accurate." I looked around the kitchen at the collateral damage from Jared's spell. "This place actually looks worse. I didn't think that was possible."

"Ready to test out your broom?" He got to his feet and offered a hand up.

"The last time you asked if I was ready, you almost killed me." I grabbed his hand, accepting his offer of help.

"The key word there being almost." Jared slipped on his shirt before picking a few shards of glass from my hair. "Come on, we've got less than an hour left."

"No pressure." I said, and followed him through the old laundry room and out the back door into a sizeable yard edged with overgrown herb gardens.

No pressure. All that was left to do was stop Helene and rescue Prudence. *No problem.*

Accept for the part where I didn't feel any different.

Chapter Eleven

"Let's see, something difficult." Jared thumbed through the pages of my family's grimoire. "Conjuring, no. Manifestations, also no. Damn it, we don't have the ingredients for any of these."

A variety of herbs and plants with medicinal purposes grew in the gardens surrounding the backyard. I knew at least half by name thanks to the hours I spent with Hector tending the Harris's gardens. Everything we needed for a multitude of spells was there for the taking but we couldn't use any of it. What plants weren't ravaged by insects and disease were choked out with weeds rendering all of it useless.

I could relate.

"Divination, too easy." Jared muttered, still searching for the right spell to test my new skills.

"I beg to differ." Nothing about divination came easy to me. My readings were fifty-fifty. Accurate enough for gas money but not enough to pay rent.

"Telepathy. That should work." Jared held out the grimoire. "Here, this one doesn't require anything but opening the third eye and tapping a ley line. Read it to yourself a few times to get the feel of it and then out loud. I want you to get inside my head."

"Your mind is not a destination location. I've seen the relics you sell and what's inside some of those jars in your workshop. The last place I want to be is inside your head."

I wasn't sure what scared me more, accessing his knowledge of the black arts or learning what Jared really thought about me.

"I don't see any ley—."

"You're using the wrong eyes to see." Jared tapped a finger against my forehead. "Stop thinking like a person and think like a witch for a change."

"For a change?" I punctuated my irritation with a one fingered salute. *Easy for him to say when magic's always come easy for him.*

"She's charming, Jared. I see why you've been keeping her all to yourself." Helene strolled through the garden gate like she was fashionably late for tea party.

"Holy Hecate." I backed up, putting a few steps between my would-be killer and myself.

"Not quite, dear. But close. Closer once I'm finished with you." Helene's smile revealed perfectly white, perfectly aligned teeth. With porcelain skin and good bone structure she was quite beautiful. Until you looked in her eyes and saw the ugliness within. "I admit, I'd lost faith in you Jared but here you are. The girl and the grimoire with minutes to spare."

For someone who was supposed to be street smart, I did a lot of stupid things – like trust Jared Adams. Again.

"And you released the bind. So thoughtful." Helene slipped off her strappy high heeled shoes and padded across the damp grass. "A deal's a deal, Adams. Hand it over."

Jared traded the book of spells and my last shot at saving Prudence for a deed and his freedom. "Ellie, it's—."

"Save it, Jared." I'd heard enough of his hollow apologies and lies. "Where's Pru? I want to see her."

Helene laughed as she flipped through the pages of the grimoire. "You're in no position to make demands, cousin. But, since this is a family reunion of sorts...."

Helene's entourage came around the side of the house with Prudence in tow. She was alive. Tears tracked down my cheeks at the sight of her. From a distance she appeared to be well kept. Her raven hair was styled in two long braids and the clothes she wore looked expensive.

But the truth became evident the closer Pru got.

Dark circles and blood shot eyes. Sunken cheeks and protruding collar bones. Telltale signs of a sleep and hunger strike. Prudence fell into Helen's trap but she refused to be used as bait to catch someone else – namely me.

"She's stubborn. A trait you both seem to share. Doesn't matter. She'll break once you're dead." Helene sounded almost giddy but her amusement didn't last long. The curve of her lips flattened to a straight line, erasing her deviant smile. Her precision plucked brows knitted together as she narrowed her eyes and zeroed in on Jared. "Where is it?"

"Where is what? The spell?" Jared shrugged. "Some pages are missing. Someone must have torn them out."

"Don't. Play. Dumb. With. Me." Helene punctuated every word as her anger increased. She waited a beat for Jared to produce the missing pages. When he failed to produce them, she tapped a line in a show of power.

How did I know that?

The answer came with the soft hum of magic in the ground beneath my feet and the illumination of every ley line running through the yard. Silver lines cut across the grass, dividing the property into equal wedges of a pie.

Holy Hecate. Jared actually did it.

Energy coursed through my veins, flushing my body with power unlike anything I'd ever known. *If Helene wants my magic, she can have it. Just not the way she expected.* When Jared unleashed my magic, the spells held within the pages of the grimoire came with it. My mother's plan to lock away all that power and knowledge to hide me from Helene didn't work. But I had a plan of my own. I just needed to buy enough time to implement it.

"You're willing to risk everything for a half-ass street trash witch?" My cousin shed her layers of refinement and revealed the dark witch beneath the designer dress. "We'll see how good your chances are now."

Helene pulled an athame from the pleats of her skirt and pressed the blade against Pru's neck. A fine trail of blood trickled down her neck. "The missing pages or she dies."

"No." I rushed forward but Jared grabbed the back of my jacket and yanked me back. Terrified Helene would kill Pru, I wriggled free of the coat and spun on Jared. "Give her the pages. I'm not going to let my sister die because of me."

"The first dreamwalker in Gaston?" Jared threw my jacket on the ground. "She's not going to hurt Prudence. She's too valuable."

"If there's one thing Jared knows, it's priceless items on the black arts market. Your sister is a rare find and it would pain me to kill her. But...." Helene pressed the athame deeper into Prudence's neck. "Her life isn't worth as much to me as your death."

"Ellie." Prudence spoke for the first time; her voice calm and even. "If you die, we all die." Her eyes held a depth of emotions – fear, sorrow, love.

The most terrifying of them all was resolve.

"Pru, no. No, no, please." I knew what she was about to do and I knew there was no way for me to stop her.

That didn't stop me from trying.

I rushed forward, hoping to knock Helene off balance and the blade from her hand. Helene didn't kill a coven of witches and survive as long as she had by being an easy target. She shoved the energy from the tapped ley line in my direction. The rush of magic hit me with enough force to leave me flat on my back gasping for air. I rolled to my side and locked eyes with my sister. Tears streamed down my cheeks as I shook my head, praying for the Goddess to intervene.

"You never stick up for yourself. Fight back, Ellie." Prudence didn't beg or plead for her life. She simply leaned forward, relaxed her muscles and let the weight of her body finish what Helene started. Pru's neck slid across the blade as her legs went out from under her.

Racked with sobs, I managed to get to my knees and crawl to my sister's side despite the weight of the grief crushing down on me. She was right, of course. I survived but I never fought. Never once stood up for myself. I was a punching bag, taking hits as they came. Barbara, school yard bullies, Jared, and now Helene. From the moment I was born, life seemed intent on knocking me down.

But I always got back on my feet and I intended to stay that way – for Pru.

Helene sidestepped the blood soaking the ground in front of her. "What a waste of a sacrifice when you're going to die anyway – with or without the spell. I'd prefer to have your powers but closing the circle works too." She raised the athame, poised to drive the blade down into my skull.

"I curse you, Helene Vonigan. I curse you to—." Jared's protest was short lived as Helene's men pummeled him into submission, dropping his bloodied, beaten body beside Pru's.

"Such devotion in such a short time. I'm impressed. Jared only ever looks out for himself. I'd consider bringing you into the fold if I didn't have to kill you. Mores the pity." Helene struck, connecting with my shoulder as I ducked my head to avoid the killing blow. "This could all be over, Ellie, if you'd just hold still."

Her men moved in, one on each side to hold me down like medieval executioners. A woman with a miniature sword took the place of an axe and chopping block. Fear and adrenaline kicked my heart into high gear, pumping more blood through the stab wound in my shoulder. A warm river of red ran down my arm, coating my fingers and eventually the ley lines.

The soft silver glow of the ley line turned bright red before fading to a pink shimmer as my blood was carried out across the grid. I never worked blood magic, or any real magic beyond tarot and simple gris-gris, but that didn't matter. I inadvertently made an offering when my blood hit the ley line – an offering that was accepted. The spells were all there inside my mind. The magic flowed through my veins.

All that was left to do was use it.

Helene's blade sliced across my cheek as I rolled out of the way. She let out a ferocious battle cry and lunged for the kill. I yanked the ley line and spooled the energy until I couldn't hold any more, pushing some of it toward Helene. She hit the ground hard enough to bounce her head off the grass. I channeled what was left of the magic into working the same spell she'd hoped to use on me. She scrambled to her knees and reached for the athame. With one hand dug into the dirt, I clawed at her ankle until I could grab hold of her foot and pull her back.

The magic flowed through me into Helene and back, completing a circuit. It was designed to siphon the power from a witch on her death bed. When used on the living, it pulled more than magic into the circuit. Helene's lifeforce and energy coated everything like an oil slick on the ocean. The darkness that made its home inside her body sought out a new residence in mine, contaminating everything it touched as it slithered around inside of me.

The spell continued to drain the life from Helene; changing my aura in the process. She writhed on the ground, fighting until her last breath and the last ounce of her wickedness transferred to me.

"Goddess, please." I cried out for help, overwhelmed with the power of the magic and evil intermixed within me.

"Ellie?" Jared stirred from unconsciousness. "Holy Hecate. Ellie."

He got to his feet and staggered over, dropping to his knees beside me. After prying my fingers from around Helene's foot, he placed my outstretched palm against the ground. "You have to force it out."

"I don't know how." I ground out through clenched teeth.

Time slipped through my fingers like grains of sand. The transformation was almost complete. I was becoming something else, something dark and deadly.

And I feared there was no going back.

Chapter Twelve

The dark magic growing within me curdled my stomach. On my knees and hunched over, I retched until it felt like my insides turned inside out. I hoped the darkness took the same route as the contents of my stomach, but it filled the void until I felt bloated and sick again. My abdominal muscles cramped while I dry heaved as the evil tried to make more room in my body.

"Ellie, it's consuming you. You have to force it out." Jared tore another strip of fabric, this time from the bottom of his shirt, and wiped my mouth.

Drenched in sweat, my clothes stuck like a second skin as a fever raged while my immune system fought to kick out the magic's parasitic invasion. It was a losing battle. The magic Helene tainted with her wickedness was going to succeed in killing me where she had failed.

Too bad she wasn't there to see it.

Jared switched from shouting at me to fight to praying for the Goddess to save me. "I'm going to see what I can find in the house to help. I'll be right back, Ellie. Just... keep fighting."

What kind of spell was this? My family was seriously screwed up if this was the type of magic they practiced. My birth mother was right – I was better off in foster care. Thoughts of family turned my mind to Pru who died so I could live.

In other words, she died for nothing.

Didn't she?

A small tremor in her right pinkie gave me hope. Prudence had a little fight left in her. *So, what's my excuse?* The possibility my sister might survive was all the motivation I needed. I scratched and clawed through the dirt until my hands were buried. Jolts of electricity carried through the lines into my fingertips. I traced the current of energy back to the source and downloaded everything I picked up from Helene into the magic network.

Once again, the light illuminating from the lines changed color from silver to black where I tapped the line, lightening again as the darkness was dispersed back into the vast pool of magic running beneath Gaston City and the ley lines across the continent.

Jared lit what was left of the candles and a small stash of sage he'd found in the kitchen. His cleansing ritual helped increase the speed of the transfer and recovery time for me and the network of magic. The crease between his brow smoothed as the line's silver hue returned. "Holy Hecate, Ellie." He cupped my face in his hands, leaned in, and pressed his lips to mine in a crushing, passionate kiss. "I thought you were going to die."

It looked like I wasn't the only one affected by my near death experiences.

I rested a hand on his chest just above his heart and pushed back from the kiss. "Prudence."

He nodded his understanding but I caught a hint of regret in his eyes, as if an opportunity had passed and he knew we'd never get it back.

Still feeling the aftereffects of Helene's magic, I decided crawling was faster than trying to stand and walk over to my sister's side. The knife wound narrowly missed the jugular. My hands shook as I reached out to check her pulse. There was blood. So much blood. And in varying stages of coagulation. Between the injury and the blood, I didn't know here to press my fingers, so I checked her wrist.

"I can't tell if she actually has a pulse or if my blood is pumping so hard I'm just feeling my own." I looked over the limp body of my sister at Jared. "Will you check?"

He nodded and moved in but the look on his face said he already knew the answer. "I don't feel.... Wait, there. It's so faint I almost missed it. How is this possible?"

"I don't care about how. I just care that it is." Overcome with emotion, tears streamed down my cheeks, falling in heavy drops.

My happiness was short lived when I saw heartache reflected back at me in Jared's eyes. "I don't think she's going to.... She doesn't have long, Ellie."

"I can fix her." I moved Jared's hand from Pru's wrist while he tried to convince me that even with magic nothing could be done to save her.

He was wrong.

The same way I knew the spell for Helene's undoing, I knew my family's spell for restoring life. My ancestors didn't walk the line between black and white magic, they tap danced right over it. But Prudence wasn't dead. Reviving her wouldn't tilt the natural balance of the world any more than a blood transfusion or those shocker paddles hospitals use.

Once again, I clawed through the grass and dirt until my right hand was completely covered in blood-soaked earth. Once again, I tapped a line. The process of giving and taking life was so similar, a simple change in direction and intent was all that the spell required.

Prudence's body reclaimed her spilled blood, down to the last drop. Every blade of grass and spec of dirt around her was cleaned until the spot where my sister died no longer existed – because her death never occurred.

Pru gasped as her eyes fluttered open. With a shaky hand she reached for her neck and gingerly touched the spot where her throat had been slit. A scar, still angry and red from where the skin knitted back together, took the place of an open wound. "Oh Ellie, you died, too?"

"I'm not dead, Pru." I brushed a few stray hairs from her eyes. "Neither are you. How do you feel?"

"Like I died." Prudence tried to sit up, apparently reconsidered, and remained on her back. "Is that the cute guy from the park? The one who was always watching you? He's your boyfriend now, huh?"

"You're chatty for someone who almost died. Don't make me regret saving you." I offered a playful warning as I wiped the tears from my eyes.

The fear and tension marring Prudence's face eased into a beautiful smile as she dozed off. Being mostly dead and then brought back to life had obviously taken its toll on her.

Jared hung back, mouth agape as he watched the sisterly banter between us. He looked confused, bewildered, and a bit scared all at once. "That's not possible. Only necromancers can do what you just did."

After reassuring Pru that she was safe, that I'd be right back, and planting a kiss on her forehead, I went over to Jared. "And we're going to keep it that way. No witch should have this spell or the one Helene was after." I held out my hand. "Where is it?"

Jared pulled a folded piece of paper from his back pocket. "You're right. It needs to be destroyed." He spoke with conviction but the look of longing in his eyes said he had a few regrets.

I took the spell before searching the backyard for the family grimoire. With the book complete, I grabbed Jared's backpack and emptied its contents on the ground. "There they are." I came up with a book of matches and took everything to a fire circle in the back corner of the yard.

"You're going to burn it?" Jared asked, following me across the yard. He sidestepped in front of me to block my path. "The whole book?"

"Yes, the whole book." I answered, noting the way he eyed the spell book with such longing. "Some day I'm going to find someone who looks at me the way you look at this grimoire."

"You already have. You just haven't noticed. I'll see if I can scrounge up some kindling." Jared took the matches and walked off toward the hedge line, saving me from my romantically awkward self. I had little experience with compliments or relationships and had no idea what to do with either.

After piling enough leaves and dry grass clippings to get a small fire going, I set the grimoire in the flames. Hungry for food, the fire devoured the old pages.

"I don't suppose you have any marshmallows in that bag of yours? I have a killer craving for sugar." Prudence placed a hand on my shoulder for stability and sat down in front of the fire pit. "It must be the blood loss." She shrugged, taking the entire experience in stride.

And that was why I had to save her. Pru was my counter weight, adding balance to an otherwise topsy-turvy life.

"It must be." I wrapped an arm around her shoulder and pulled her in close. "We're almost finished. I just need to make sure this is done and then I'll take you back to the house."

"I don't think I want to go back." Pru stared off into what remained of the fire.

"That's a fight for another day. I'm no help where Barbara's concerned. You're on your own for that one." I was only half joking.

Pru knew I had her back but bringing me along would only hurt her case. After all, I was the reason she went missing in the first place. And while Barbara Harris would never know the truth, she'd sure as hell find a way to pin it on me anyway.

"I still don't see why we had to burn the whole grimoire." Jared stomped out the last of the embers. There was nothing left of my family's spells but ash.

"Everything worth putting down on paper is right here." I assured him, tapping my right temple. "I'm sure I can find a journal or something that I like at Cauldron Crafts. I know the owner so I get a discount."

One corner of his mouth upturned in a wry smile. "Oh, I'm sure I'll have something to your liking."

"You had to go and make it awkward." Pru elbowed Jared in the ribs before linking her arm through mine. "I guess it's time."

"How much do you think an Uber would cost from here to the Heights? My treat." I walked away from my ancestral home with my sister on one arm and Jared on the other.

Seeing Barbara Harris again ranked somewhere around root canal with no Novocain. I was in no hurry for either. But I survived a crazy witch hell bent on killing me, rescued my sister, and learned a little about myself and my family in the process – I could survive my former foster mother.

Maybe.

· · · ·

"I HAD ANOTHER DREAM." Pru padded barefoot into the kitchen and stole my cup of coffee.

"That's considered an act of war in some countries." I said as I got up to pour myself another cup. "Was I in the dream?"

"No." She smiled over the rim of the mug. "But *he* was. Come on, Ellie. You know you want to know. His intentions are good."

From her teasing tone, I knew she meant Jared. The fact that my sister dreamt of a possible, sort of maybe romantic interest of mine would have been unnerving if she wasn't a dreamwalker.

Actually, that made it more unnerving.

"You know what Mark Twain said about good intentions." I took a sip of my coffee. "The road to Hell is paved with them."

I fought the temptation to ask for details. Sometimes it's better not to know.

Besides, the last time I asked, I regretted it. The images were seared into my brain and no matter how hard I tried I couldn't scrub them out. The dream involved a young boy, a necromancer if her description was accurate, who killed things so he could bring them back to life. He was alone, came into his powers without anyone to help him and developed a taste for death. If he stayed on his current path, he'd evolve into something dark, something more frightening and dangerous than Helene.

Prudence wanted to help him. I wanted to help Pru unlock her full potential. Neither of us were ready to play the hero.

In place of capes and matching jumpsuits, we each had a journal. Pru wrote down her dreams and I wrote down my family's spells – the ones safe for prying eyes should it end up outside of my possession. For the foreseeable future that would have to do.

Maybe one day we could pursue her dream of using her abilities to help others. But sometimes you have to save yourself before you can save someone else.

Self-care, right?

Less than a month had passed since we almost died at the hands of the psychotic, magic hungry witch who happened to be my cousin. Prudence stood up to Barbara, declared her independence, and moved in with me. They'd yet to cancel her allowance which was helpful because the James family home needed a lot of work.

The broken windows were boarded up and shards of glass swept away. The doors hung crooked on the hinges and the floorboards creaked where the foundation sagged but it was home – and it was ours. We had a roof over our heads and the privacy to discover who and what we truly are.

A witch and a dreamwalker.

The End

• • • •

Thanks for reading!
If you enjoyed Ellie's story, you'll love my Touch of Ink Series.
http://bit.ly/touchofinkseries

• • • •

About the Author

RACHEL RAWLINGS WAS born and raised in the Baltimore Metropolitan area and has always had a fascination with the strange and unusual. Although her passion for writing developed early on, it wasn't until 2009 that she published her first novel - to prove a point to her children. When she isn't writing Urban Fantasy or Paranormal Romance, Rachel can be found with her nose buried in a good book and a cup of coffee nearby. There may or may not be cookies!

Read More from Rachel Rawlings

www.rachelrawlings.com

Don't miss out!

Visit the website below and you can sign up to receive emails whenever Rachel Rawlings publishes a new book. There's no charge and no obligation.

https://books2read.com/r/B-A-CBSB-EJKEB

Did you love *Any Witch Way You Can*? Then you should read '*Ink It Over* by Rachel Rawlings!

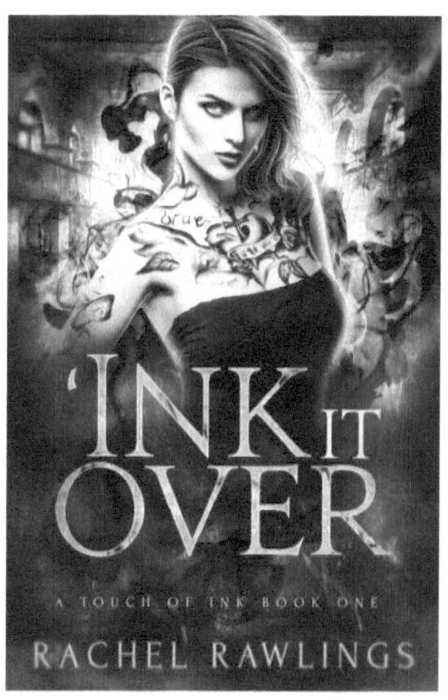

Adeline Severance leads a dangerous, magical double life.

Tattoo artist by day and warding witch by night, Adeline uses magical inks, a tattoo machine, and the help of her best friend Lars to permanently imbue spells of protection onto her clients. Thanks to the Magistrate's greed and failure to protect its citizens, her services were in high demand.

But when Nicholas Marks walks through the door of her tattoo studio looking for an appointment, one of Adeline's wards isn't the only thing he's after. Forced into working for the Magistrate, he's been tasked with bringing her in.

With her cover story blown, Adeline has two choices: Run as far and as fast as she can, or stay and fight. Though she's not ready to give up the only life she's ever known, putting her trust in a traitor may end up being the worst decision she's ever made.

Fans of The Hollows Series, Charmed and The Craft are sure to devour this series from Rachel Rawlings.

Buy 'Ink It Over to start a magic and mayhem filled adventure today!

Adeline Severance leads a dangerous, magical double life.

Tattoo artist by day and warding witch by night, Adeline uses magical inks, a tattoo machine, and the help of her best friend Lars to permanently imbue spells of protection onto her clients. Thanks to the Magistrate's greed and failure to protect its citizens, her services were in high demand.

But when Nicholas Marks walks through the door of her tattoo studio looking for an appointment, one of Adeline's wards isn't the only thing he's after. Forced into working for the Magistrate, he's been tasked with bringing her in.

With her cover story blown, Adeline has two choices: Run as far and as fast as she can, or stay and fight. Though she's not ready to give up the only life she's ever known, putting her trust in a traitor may end up being the worst decision she's ever made.

Fans of The Hollows Series, Charmed and The Craft are sure to devour this series from Rachel Rawlings.

Buy 'Ink It Over to start a magic and mayhem filled adventure today!

Read more at www.rachelrawlings.com.

Also by Rachel Rawlings

The Jax Rhoades Series
Payable on Death
Paid in Full

The Maurin Kincaide Series
The Morrigna
Witch Hunt
Wolfsbane
Blood Bath
Ill Fated
Darkness Hunts
Mistletoe Meltdown
The Maurin Kincaide Series Box Set
The Maurin Kincaide Series Box Set

Standalone
Sherri 2.0
Any Witch Way You Can

Watch for more at www.rachelrawlings.com.